The Legacy of the Limehouse Link

Daniel A. Anthony

authorHOUSE®

AuthorHouse™ UK
1663 Liberty Drive
Bloomington, IN 47403 USA
www.authorhouse.co.uk
Phone: UK TFN: 0800 0148641 (Toll Free inside the UK)
*   UK Local: (02) 0369 56322 (+44 20 3695 6322 from outside the UK)*

Published by AuthorHouse 10/06/2021

ISBN: 978-1-6655-9369-4 (sc)
ISBN: 978-1-6655-9368-7 (e)

DEDICATION

To my grandson and granddaughter, for being the final piece to life's perfect gig-saw.

CONTENTS

ACKNOWLEDGEMENTS

My thanks to Dr.Valery Kuan. Without her help, I would never have become acquainted to the three sisters. To Karen Crane for all the help. And finally to Nana, for bringing it all together.

FOREWORD

It's not for the want of a tongue that a cow cannot talk.
And why do we want to run, before we can walk?
The mysteries of life are not always what we think.
The same rules apply to the Limehouse link.

CHAPTER 1

THE LIMEHOUSE LINK

It was the saddest sight you could ever imagine. The hearse, the one car, the priest, and one old lady. I would definitely not go out of the world like that. I would insist on hiring from "Rent-a-Crowd". I must write that in my will, just in case.

Having worked for a small-town newspaper as a hack and moved to a part time reporter, I could sniff there might be a story in it, you know. Why, after all his life, was there not one person, apart from his wife, or mother (or girlfriend) to see him off? Of course, I was assuming a lot. I did not know if it was a man being buried and it might have been his sister, again assuming that it was a man!

Now I was there to see off an old friend - well he used to be an old friend - who did have a family. Three sisters, nieces, nephews, aunts, uncles, cousins, more family than he knew he had. They had crawled out of every hole imaginable, all hoping they'd be left something, all there to fight over a will.

I suppose that poor sod being buried over there didn't have a will or anything to leave, otherwise he'd have had people crawling all over the place just like the mob. It'll be fun having the will being read out. Stuart Graham had a wicked sense of humour and he knew that he was going to die. He knew it wouldn't be long before all the people he had ever cheated, forced out of business would be there at his funeral. Most of them would have killed him just to be at his funeral. Somebody there did. But who?

I'm sure there will be some surprises as to who gets what and who did what!

Stuart Graham had asked to be buried at Chingford near to Ronnie Kray. I don't know if he knew the twins. They certainly weren't friends of his. He didn't have any friends, just like the poor sod over there looks like he had no friends either - of course, that's assuming it is, or was he!

By this time the small cortege across the way, had departed. So I thought that I would slope off and see if there were any clues as to who had been buried.

Sure enough there was a message written on a card stuck into the single wreath near to the hole with the coffin inside. All it said was "From your Favourite Flowers".

That's all it said. It didn't have the decency to say "Good Luck Tom, Charlie, and With Love from whomever. Nothing -just "From Your Favourite Flowers".

Stuart's lot were making their way back to their cars. We were all meeting up at a posh restaurant in Woodford near to where Stuart had his large mansion in Chigwell. Looking back to the Lone Ranger's grave, I bet that poor sod did not have a mansion. I bet he didn't have a pot to... to put his ashes in. That's why they buried him. That is, if it was a him.

I just had to know who was in that grave. I'd noticed the name of the undertakers was the same firm as Stuart's, Frank Walkers from the Commercial Road. So it was not going to be much trouble finding out. I mingled with the crowd returning to the limo's, got near to the driver of one of the cars and nonchalantly said "Your firm's busy. I see you buried the chap opposite" "Yes", he said, "things are looking up or down whichever way you look at it" and quickly turned away and got into the driver's seat.

Unless I was mistaken the driver was hiding something, there was something going on, not quite right. For a large man he seemed almost scared. He certainly didn't want to talk about the funeral. Just then I was grabbed from behind, in fact it was my behind. "Hello", she said, "I thought that was you" "Well, if it wasn't me, it was someone else" "Well, if it had not been you, it would have been someone else, and I would have made a stranger very happy"

"You're not with her, are you?" - referring to my ex-partner Cathy. "No, we split some time ago when I ran out of money" "Who are you kidding, you never had any money." "That's right, but she did!" I answered.

This was Stuart Graham's half-sister, Meigui. I knew her from way back. We went to the same school, Farance Street, just off Burdett Road. Stuart Graham was not his true name. His mother never knew his father's real name. She discovered herself pregnant when she was sixteen. Whilst at a friend's birthday party, she got more than friendly with a boy named Stuart or Graham - she wasn't sure, and that's how he got his name!

His mother, Judith, was kicked out of her home. Her father would have nothing to do with her. She got a job as a barmaid, at Charlie Brown's pub, officially known as the Railroad Tavern. Judith Ashbolt was a good looking girl and looked older than the 16 years 11 months she was when Stuart was born. She was well liked by everybody at the quite famous pub, universally known at 'Charlie Browns' which stood on the corner of Garford St and West Ferry Road. It was convenient for her since she had rented a room above the Golden Dragon Chinese restaurant, better known as up the step's, and finished up marrying the owner Mr Chang. So you get the story. After 10 years Mr Chang died and left all his money to Stuart's mum, Judith Ashbolt, who later died tragically and Stuart finished up with all the money, restaurants and had all of the 'Chang's' estate, which was a number of properties, in and around London. And now, with Stuart having no offspring, who gets the loot / dough.

"I didn't think my charming brother had so many friends," said Meigui. "I didn't think he had any at all' I replied and added "so I've heard". "What are you doing here?" she said. "Stuart requested it" I answered and added "I thought I'd let bygones be bygones".

It was easy. Looking back over the years, they were good times. The 3 of us, me Danny Holmes, Stuart and his scrawny sister, Meigui. In 1950s East London, long before the Limehouse Link, our world was roughly 3 square miles from the West India Docks, Isle of Dogs, Canning Town, Victoria Park and downtown towards the West End of London, Limehouse. We didn't choose where we were born, but you are what you are. You grew up in a rough, tough and dirty area, where most people lived and worked in poverty. . There was only one way to go, up. Well that is not exactly correct, the more up I went, meant that I owed more money, so I suppose up means you're moving up the borrowing ladder, in my case, not a lot of chance of paying any of it back.

The name Limehouse, seems to come from lime oats, another name for kilns, and when we were young, Stuart, me and Meigui used to hang around playing, living in those dirty streets with names like Limehouse Causeway, Three Colts St, Narrow Street, and Penny fields, not knowing anything about the prostitutes, opium dens and pukapoo Chinese gambling dens, most of which had long ago ceased to exist. I did not know but they had been run by Meigui's family "the Changs", and that all the proceeds had been handed down to Stuart Graham.

Meigui must have been thinking about along the same lines as myself and as we got close, we just had to hug each other, but drew away quickly as we both realised my youth had been renewed.

"You never could hide your feelings." Don't kid yourself' I said, "It's my car keys"

"What you holding in your hand then?" "Putting my car keys in my coat pocket," I changed the subject and said "There's a lot here isn't there?" looking at all the cars that were filling up. "There's a lot there" she said, teasing me, and enjoying embarrassing me, which she always had a knack of doing. "Drop it" I stammered.

"I haven't seen you for years and straight away you're asking me to drop things. Anyhow I'm not wearing any...." she said, still teasing. Getting away from that conversation, I said, "Did you see the burial opposite, there was only one person attending." "Didn't notice," she said and kissing my cheek added "Catch up with you later" and rushed away.

What is it about that bloke over there, is there something? Everybody knows but is not saying.

We arrived at the 'Prince Regent' and, after parking the car. I followed behind a group of people into this rather plush hallway with a large staircase and outsized chandeliers leading to the banqueting rooms. The gathering had split into two groups, a rowdy crowd which had to be Stuart's lot and the Chinese who had gathered near the far end of the room. I saw a few faces I knew from way back in Stuart's lot, so I made for a completely bald headed man that I knew called 'Downdrough'.

"Hello Downdrough" I said, "it's been a long time" holding out my hand for him to shake. Grabbing my hand he said "Danny Holmes, I thought you'd turn up. Glad to see you Danny. You remember Danny, don't you Diane" "hello Dan," said Diane.

I looked at Diane, and again become somewhat embarrassed, and mumbled "Hi Di" and heard myself saying "you're still gorgeous, the last time I saw you was in the 'White Horse' Burdett Road, up on the stage singing - don't tell me - no wait - I got it - 'Kiss, kiss me.' You looked like Marilyn but sounded better" and "couldn't that Jimmy Fags play those ivories."

Somebody grabbed me from behind, I swung round "Holmey" you? Wherever you been, I've not seen you for yonks." "Nibbo Wilson! Well I'll go back to our house; I've still got the bruises on my legs. Did you ever get around to kicking the ball?"

"You know they banned me for life, for kicking the bleeding ref" "Why doesn't that surprise me?

How's your brother Charlie, did they ban him for kicking?" "Well not quite, they sent him down for kicking the bucket." Everybody fell about laughing, which raised some eyebrows from the other end of the room.

At that time somebody rapped on a table and a voice could be heard saying "Can I have your attention please". There was a hush and it all went quiet. "As the attorney of the late Mr Stuart Graham, I have been left instructions by him, I would like you all to raise your glasses in memory of Mr Stuart Graham" - which we all did. - "before I read out the last will and testament of Mr Graham"

"It says to Danny Holmes I leave my possessions, property, money and bonds, along with all other interests, in fact I leave everything, and that means everything, to you Danny Holmes and hope it brings you more happiness than it brought me".

The only person not to hear this was me. I had quickly run out to the toilet. So, as I returned, I entered the room and every single person in that room turned and stared in my direction. The attorney, Mr Davidson-Smyth, called for the attention of everybody and continued, "I have further instructions for Mr Holmes for which I feel now is not the appropriate time" and, gesturing to me to come forward, offered his hand and said "let me be the first to congratulate you Mr Holmes. I look forward to continue to work for you and your companies if you so desire it"

"What are you talking about?" I said, withdrawing my hand; "What's going on? Is this some kind of joke?" "No Mr Holmes. Mr Graham has legally left you everything. If you come to my office, which is of course your office as you own it, I will go through all the paperwork you will need to sign. I suggest you get yourself a third party solicitor to act on your behalf before signing anything."

He then handed me a large envelope.

I stood there in a daze. I heard Meigui offering me a drink and taking it from her, I looked into her eye's and my memory took over, back to when we were kids -.me, Stuart and his scrawny little half-sister Meigui. We went everywhere together. Life seemed so much easier and simple in those days, the 1960s, everybody still picking themselves up from the war years and getting on with their lives.

Kids could roam the streets for hours, getting into and out of trouble, all of the time. Grown-up people could tell you off and we would take notice - the biggest threat would be that they would tell your parents. The three of us were always being told off, buzz off or words to that effect. But it did not deter us. We would climb through small holes in the fences into the dockyards and play for hours, dodging behind cargos in and out of sheds. Everybody seemed so busy. We could come and go as we pleased. Stuart and I were about eight and Meigui was 6 or 7. She seemed to be with us constantly. Even when the gang grew, Meigui was around. She became one of the boys - so much so as I never treated her as anything else - until that fateful day some years later.

We had decided to go to Greenwich Park this time. Meigui was 15, and I was 17. We and the gang jumped on the 56 bus at the "Eastern", past West India Docks gates. We were all shouting and larking around, passing all the sights that was our world, around the walls, on past Morton's, John Lenanton's wood yard, onto the Millwall dock gates, across the iron bridge, past the old Presbyterian church - this used to be our youth club - past the fire station, onto 'the gardens' where we jumped off the bus. I can remember so well. We had done it many, many times before. We made our way to the Greenwich foot tunnel under the Thames, shouting and laughing. We caught the lift up from the tunnel and, as we came out, the sun seemed so strong. I looked at Meigui and it flashed through my mind how lovely she looked. And I thought no more about it.

'The old 'Cutty Sark' was full of tourists and we made our way up to the top of Greenwich Park hill. What a beautiful day! Everything was fresh, sunny and free. Looking down over London was breath-taking; there were still signs of destruction like burnt-out buildings, large debris patches where building and houses used to stand. But this was not a day to be moping and looking back. This was a glorious sunny day for being alive. Why did I feel this good?

Meigui and I was out-stepping the other three. Stuart, Nibbo and his brother Charlie, were lagging behind, trying to attract the attention of three girls who were trying to attract their attention but making out (not convincingly) that nothing was going on.

They were lagging so far behind, we decided to sit down and wait for them to catch up.

Meigui seemed strangely quiet. So, after a while, I said we should go back down and find the others. "Come on scrawny" I said, "up you get" and put out my hand to help her up. In that short moment my life changed. In fact it began. She grabbed hold of my hand and we both fell over. I stretched out with my other hand to save her and grabbed her bodice which came open and I finished up on top of her, looking down on a beautiful body.

My eyes wandered up and met Meigui's which meant that I did not react to her hand which slapped me around the face "What was that for?" I said. "That's for staring at me," she said, with her cheeks becoming slightly red. "I couldn't help it" I said, adding "I've seen you a hundred times, when we were swimming." "That was a long time ago," she replied and I realised it had been over 10 years ago since we all swam, just in our pants, off the Limehouse Reach. "And don't call me scrawny again," she said, doing up her last button which didn't want doing up.

She had become a beautiful young woman without me noticing her. She was no longer a scrawny little kid that we'd dragged around for the last 10 years. The tomboy had grown up. I realised why I was feeling good all day, but things don't last.

We started to walk down the hill, saw the others and decided to make our way back home. Meigui and I kept well apart from each other, and, as we were climbing the stairs, of the Greenwich tunnel, instead of taking the lift back to the surface at the Isle of Dogs side, I quickly became embarrassed when I found myself looking at parts of Meigui's body that

I had never noticed before. She was glancing back, catching me looking. She knew I could not take my eyes off her, but we could not dare to look each other in the eyes.

What we did not notice was that Stuart was watching our every move.

We all jumped off the bus at 'Charlie Browns' and 'Nibbo' and his brother Charlie, crossed over West Ferry Road and, turning around at the corner of Penny Fields, said that we'd meet in the morning for football training.

Stuart didn't like football so I asked him to meet us after. Meigui went straight into the Chinese restaurant where they lived above. Out of the blue Stuart said to me "Danny, you're looking at my sister differently and I don't like what's going on." I assured him that there was nothing going on, which there wasn't. "Well that's OK, but there better not be. Her family wouldn't allow it."

But Meigui had different ideas and had already decided that I was going to be the man in her life, no matter what Stuart, her family or anybody else including me thought. Of course all this came to a head about 3 months after we fell for each other in Greenwich Park. Our first meeting came about when Meigui slipped a note into my hand, saying we had to meet and talk. A time, a date was set. Secretly we had agreed to meet at the Troxy Cinema in Commercial Road. To this day I could not tell you what film was showing. We only had eyes for each other. I remembered walking her home or near her house. And I'll always remember our first kiss.

The mist faded and I was back at Stuart's funeral.

I must have been a million miles away, looking into Meigui's eyes and hearing her say "My brother always had a wicked sense of humour, but this time he has gone too far". Pausing, she added "You knew all about this, didn't you. You and Stuart planned it all".

"I can assure you, this is the first I have heard of it. There must be some mistake". I said.

Stuart's attorney, Mr Davidson-Smythe, butted in. "I can assure you, Mr Holmes, Mr Graham left strict instructions, in the presence of me and two witnesses, that every last penny would be left to you. He, Mr Graham, said that you would know his reasons behind this remarkable gift. He also told me to tell you to be wary about the flowers. I must confess the remarks concerning the flowers made no sense to me."

"What did you say about flowers", I said, thinking about the Lone Ranger's message on one wreath, "From - your favourite flowers." Was there some connection? I made a mental note to find out who it was in the other grave. What does Stuart mean, be wary about the flowers? I wonder if he means 'Poppies', relating to drugs.

Or did he refer to three local lads, all homosexuals, Stuart's cousin, his stepfather's brother's boy who we called 'Daisy' being his surname was Chang and his two friends, Joe 'Lillie' Langtree, 'Lillie', it could not be anything else with Langtree as his surname, and 'Pansy', would you believe 'Potter', well you'd be wrong. His name was Kevin Brown. We just always called him 'Pansy', I never did know why.

Meigui wasn't at all pleased and the Chinese lot down the other end of the room had forgotten their good behaviour stance and were becoming rather agitated and noisy, arguing amongst each other. Of course, we at this end could not understand their language but their body language was becoming rather offensive, things were becoming rather heated so you know what I did, when the heat gets too much get out of the kitchen and thinking that I would not like to end up as Number 6 on the menu (that's for starters), I asked the attorney for his business card and said that I would ring him. I told Nibbo to tell all my old mates who was there, to arrange to get together at the old local, "The Eastern Hotel". "It's no longer there, Holmesy, leave it to me and I'll arrange something, you'd better get going", and off I went.

Christ these boys work quick. I arrived at my car and all the tyres had been spiked.

At that moment, Meigui pulled up in her car and told me to get in - it was the second best offer I'd had that day so I jumped in beside her. Looking her up and down, I realised that she had not lost whatever it was that I'd always desired, so I told her 'You haven't changed a bit, as good as gold, full of eastern promise. You were always there when it counts." "You think so, do you, it was me who spiked your tyres"? "What did you do that for"? "I wanted to get my hands on your car keys", she said, referring to our earlier conversation.

I'd been away for a long time, I suppose too long. And now, back in my old back yard, everywhere I looked was bringing back memories, emotions, good times and bad times. Nostalgia isn't good for you; you have to get on with 'now'. But how can I forget. Meigui and I had been going steady after our first date at the Troxy for about six months, secretly meeting whenever we could. We were so much in love, and it should have been the happiest time of our young lives. But then her family found out. Stuart's mum, Meigui's stepmother, stopped me in the street and told me there was no way we could go on seeing each other, her father, Mr Chang, would not allow it. He did not want Meigui to marry anyone who was not a Chinaman. She understood why I might find this hypocritical, him, Mr Chang, marrying her, an English girl of Irish parents, but pointed out that Meigui and her two sisters, Xiang Ju and Mudan were Chinese women by his first wife, who died when Meigui was born . So the elders of the family would not allow the marriage. Judith Ashbolt (Mrs Chang) begged us to obey their wishes and warned me of some terrible outcome if we would not stop seeing each other.

I noticed that we were just approaching Blackwall Tunnel, and I had been so locked up in my thoughts that I lost count of where I was. But why were we going through the tunnel?

"Meigui", I said, "where are you taking me"?

"Can't you guess"?

Of course I could guess - "Greenwich Park".

"Right first time" she laughed out.

"What are we going there for" I asked.

"Confucius says it's not for the want of a tongue that a cow can't talk".

"Did Confucius say that", I asked.

"I don't know", she said.

"What does it mean"?

"Anything you want it to mean - in this case, it means shut up, and you'll find out when we get there".

"Did this Confucius guy ever stop making up sayings"?

"I think he did it to confuse people" she said, and added "that's how he got his name".

"Well I'm confused. Why did Stuart leave me all his worldly goods"?

"That's what I, and a lot of others, want to know" said Meigui. "That Mr what's-his-name Smyth, said you would know his reasons", she added, looking at me as if she fully expected me to tell her.

My silence told her I was not ready to tell her, or I did not really know what reasons Stuart was talking about. We arrived at Greenwich Park, and parked up.

"You know the last time I came here was all those years ago when you fell in my arms"."I did not fall, you were trying to rip my clothes off" she was teasing me again.

"You know that's not true" I said, "where exactly was it"?

"I come back here lots of times and I'm quite sure that just about here is where I, we, sat down".

"Who would have thought that London would rise up like that" she said, pointing to the new landscape or skyline full of tall funny shaped buildings.

"I wonder what Confucius would have said about the change, how about that glass building?"

"Confucius says man who lives in glass houses should not get undressed in front of windows, or how about if you ever go back over old ground, be wary about the flowers", I said.

"Where did that come from" Meigui asked.

"I don't know, Mr what's-his-name Smyth said Stuart warned me to be wary of the flowers. Make any sense to you?"

"There wasn't much what Stuart did or said made much sense to me" she answered.

"You know that if it wasn't for the army and conscription I would have whisked you off to somewhere abroad, so that we could have been together. Why didn't you wait for me"?

"I had to obey my family" she said, "or they would have sent me to China, which they finished up doing".

"You know they had me beat up when I tried to see you, and being they're supposed to be the oldest civilisation in the world you'd think they'd be more civilised. I wonder what old Confucius would have said about that, probably something like man who messes with Chinese beauty incurs the wrath of Chinese booty".

Meigui said 'do you have to turn everything into a joke'?

"No", I replied and added "the humour hides my nervousness. And that, what's-his-name Smyth, makes me nervous. How long has he worked for Stuart", I asked.

"He is the Chang family lawyer. Their headquarters are based in Hong

Kong I think and they've been in existence long before the Limehouse Link. And I don't mean the tunnel under the Limehouse Basin" Meigui replied.

"Confucius said the world is growing smaller". Which is a contradiction of words, but my world, which used to be three miles square, has just outgrown itself. Is what's-his-name Smyth about to tell me that I own properties abroad"?

"As far away as Thailand, Manila in fact. The four corners of the Earth. My big brother Stuart kept it a secret right up until he knew he was dying. That's when he introduced what's-his-name Smyth".

"How long have you been back"?

"Over ten years, when my husband died. I have two kids who wanted to stay with their father's parents in China. Myself, I couldn't get away soon enough."

"What about your sisters?"

"Xiang Ju and Mu Dan. Both their marriages failed. They are back in England".

"It's about time we got going", I said, getting up off the grass and quickly added "mind you don't fall this time".

"You mind where you put your hands and keep your eyes off my". To stop her from saying more, I just had to kiss her.

"What did you do that for" she asked.

"The last time you were here you slapped me".

"If you don't kiss me some more I'll slap you again".

"What would Confucius say about that" I said.

"Can we talk about more important items"?

"Like what" I enquired. "Like are you prepared to be the head of a very large organisation that you know nothing about".

"How did Stuart cope" I asked. "Get in the car and I'll tell you what happened" said Meigui. "Where are we going?

"Chigwell, to Stuart's place, or"?

"Or what"?

"I was going to say your house, now".

"Did Stuart leave anything to anyone else". I asked. "Old what's-his-name Smyth read out that before Stuart died, he'd arranged an on-going allowance to us, his sisters".

"I didn't hear any of that, I left the hall and went to the boys room, and returned, everybody looked at me then old what's-his-name Smyth congratulated me and asked me if I wanted him to carry on handling Stuart's businesses, if you follow my gist".

It didn't take long arriving in Chigwell, on up through the village, up the hill pass the pub, to the large houses, turning right into Latchmere Road, on pass a few more leafy fronted houses with in and out drive ins. It reminded me of 'High Society', and then, "Wow, who lives in a house like this" I said.

"Stuart did" Meigui answered and added "all on his own, and I don't want to hear about what Confucius has to say about that". I looked away and made no comment.

"You knew him more than anyone when we were young. You were his..." her voice trailed off, "you did everything..." the voice was trailing off again, "together". "He wasn't gay was he, I mean you're not".

I butted in, "No I'm not gay, and you know I'm not".

"Is that why, what's-her-name, Cathy, is that why she left you?" Meigui could not miss a chance to embarrass me and quickly added "you're not Danielle at the weekends, are you". We were at the door to the house. Meigui had the keys, opened the door and popped the keys back in her pocket.

"Come on in and make yourself at home. By the way, you've got two lodgers, make that three, counting me", and, shouting out loud wanting to be heard said "come on down girls look who has come to tea". Down the stairs they came, Xiang Ju and Mudan, and stood next to their sister Meigui. Although middle aged they looked like Chinese versions of Charlie's (Changs) Angels - Christ, I never remembered them looking like this. "What did Stewart leave you" I asked, and added "a fashion shop"? Mudan answered "No, a factory. Mine is dresses, Meigui, coats and accessories and Xiang Ju, Lingerie. "Would you like to see" she asked, and they all started fiddling buttons. "No, I'll take your word for it" and they all laughed out loud.

I needed a strong drink and asked 'did he have a bar somewhere'? "Let's go into the green room" said Meigui, leading the way and we all followed.

We went into this large panelled room with large French doors, looking into a fantastic garden. I couldn't see a bar anywhere until Meigui pressed a button and panels opened, showing a well-stocked bar. We got our drinks and sat down. Xiang Ju was the first to talk.

"Why did Stuart leave everything to you" she asked. "Stuart's attorney said that you would know the reason" (Silence). "So why"?

"I haven't worked it out yet". I lied.

"You don't have to accept it all" Mudan said.

"We could come to some arrangement, take a salary to you for life".

"Why should I bother with a tent when I can have the whole circus", I replied quickly.

"I think Danny's right" Meigui interrupted and added "he should at least find out what is expected of him. We only know part of what Stuart told us he did, and he only told us what he wanted us to know.

I piped in "Tell me all you know and what is expected from you, with regards to your factories". Xiang Ju, being the eldest, took the lead.

"When I became 18, it was decided that I would be sent to work in Hong Kong. I had left School, Coborne Girls, with a good education and Papa knew people in Hong Kong. He arranged a good job with a generous salary and off I went. What I found out a short time ago was that it was decided I would start from the bottom, and learn the lingerie trade from the beginning. I was taught at first how to cut the fine satin silks and cotton materials to make some of the finest underwear and nightgowns. I was steadily taught how to create patterns, make butterflies and other designs out of the neat expensive French lace by folding the lace and pinning it to sheer satin and fine nylon materials, ready for the sample machinists who would delicately sew the lace and materials together. I would then take home dozens of articles to cut around the stitches and after hours snipping away with especially small scissors, would return to the factory to press and pack and send them around the world to the largest stores and fashion shops. After a few hard years with steady progress, I moved from the shop floor to the head of department and even enjoyed travelling around the world, showing and sometimes even modelling the garments.

I never knew that after all that hard work I actually was the owner until Stuart became ill and was told that he was dying. He told us that our father, or somebody else, had decided each of our futures Mudan was to learn the dress and fashion trade, Meigui coats and accessories and myself the lingerie trade. When we found out, we did not know whether to laugh or cry and now we find out that you have been left with an empire, without doing a thing, and you are not family, how can this be?

Silence……..

Of course by this time, I had remembered, but I could not tell the sisters or anyone else. The memories came flooding back; I had not seen Stuart since 1970. Then about 20 years ago I was in Hong Kong with my ex. Cathy, when we entered a bar, we did not realize until we had ordered the drinks that it was a "Gay" bar. I remember saying to Cathy, we'd better get out of here in case somebody sees me, and thinks I'm gay. We drank up quick and made for the door and who do I bump into, yes it was Stuart, with make-up and all the gear, with another guy holding his arm, so as not to lose him. Stuart pushed me to one side and said "please Danny, don't say anything "and pressed a card into my hand and said quietly, "phone me". The next day I phoned him and we arranged to meet and in due course, we met, "good to see you", I said, and went to hug him, like old friends do, but pulled away. "Good to see you Danny", he said. It was me who was embarrassed and trying to find the right words, "I was your best friend for years, we grew up together, like brothers, why didn't you confide in me?" I added quietly, "I'm sorry Stuart, its none of my business". "Like I said, Danny, it's good to see you, and I did try to tell you a hundred times, but never found the right time."

"Is that why you never phoned me back?"

"I could never reach you, you were too busy, so I left you lots of messages, but you never bothered." Until that one call about the alibi you asked me to tell the police, that you were with me", and after that nothing, no phone call, letter, explanation not a word", "that was 10 years ago".

"I shouldn't have put in that situation, I'm sorry" he said. "And so you should be, I checked you out, and discovered you step-dad had died in the fire, when his restaurant, with your home above, burnt down with him in it. "Were you responsible?"

"You've got to believe me Danny it was an accident, I was there, and we had a fight, he was going to tell my mother that I was GAY. So I hit him with a large wok which was full of fat, and it caught fire, the flames spread so fast, I could not save, or help him, and I ran. That's when I phoned you and asked you to cover for me".

"Was there anybody else who saw you on the night of the fire?"

I asked", yes there was" he replied," who?" I asked getting agitated.

"Meigui" Stuart answered "I think" he added.

And continuing he said "we had a row, a bad one, it was two days after the fire, and she was annoyed about my mum being left everything in the will".

After a short time he said, "Are you going to turn me in Danny?"

"I can't now Stuart, it's been too long, and anyhow I'm sure it was an accident, just like you said. Let's forget all about it, shall we".

"Thanks Danny, I owe you one, and I shan't forget it."

Meigui was whispering to her sisters and by their remarks I could guess that she was telling them that Stuart was gay. "You'll be making it up" said Xiang Ju, and turning to me said "How long have you known, Danny, you're not one of them as well are you?"

"No I'm not one of them, as you put it, and I've known for a number of years".

"And that's why you were in the will, because you kept Stuart's Secret" said Mudan.

It fitted the picture so I agreed with her, and said "above all things, Stuart did not want anyone to know, especially you three, his sisters and as I have not seen any of you since I discovered, - "he was Gay", it was not hard to keep it to myself.

Meigui was quite upset at that point and said "I wonder if that's why he did not want us to get together, he fancied you for himself, it was him who must have told my parents."

We finished our drinks and drifted down memory lane, laughed until we all cried, talking about the poor old days, remembering the old characters. The good old days, we all agreed, was really bloody awful, but carefree - but what of the future?

Someone mentioned the time, and brought us back to reality, and it was time for the girls to poke a bit of fun at me, and Mudan said "There are only three bedrooms in this house, and they're already taken, so where are you sleeping Danny?

"I'll sleep on the sofa, thank you" I replied,

"You can sleep with me if you want" said Meigui.

"You had your chance years ago and you blew it" said Xiang Ju "so he can sleep with me" she said laughingly.

"I was the first to think of where Danny's sleeping, so he's sleeping with me" said Mudan.

"I've got a coin, we'll toss for it" said Meigui.

"What about all sleeping in one bed" said Xing Ju?

"I've a better idea" I said "I'm going home, call me a cab"

"There's no need for that" said Meigui and added "the sofa doubles as a bed" but couldn't help herself by adding, "you can borrow my satin pyjamas, and you like satin against your skin, as I recall.

"There's no need for that, I'll take the sofa, and before you ask, I'm not tucking anyone in - so good night. Just make sure you lock your doors because I walk in my sleep - good night girls it's been a great reunion."

That night was the first night I'd fallen to sleep counting pound notes and not sheep, I wonder just how much I've been left. I would soon find out.

CHAPTER 2

AN EMPEROR'S RANSOM

Ireached in my pocket and pulled out Davidson-Smyth's card and rang his number, "Allo, Davidson-Smyth speaking."

"Danny Holmes here."

"Where do you want to meet Mr Holmes, at your office, or maybe lunch at the Connaught Hotel, in South Audley Street?"

"How far is the office from there?"

"Just around the corner in Mount Row, about what time Mr Holmes, shall I arrange for a car to pick you up?"

"No, I'll make my own way there, about 1 o'clock."

"Very well Mr Holmes, 1 o'clock".

Sitting in the cab on the way up town, I felt very nervous. I had decided to meet Jonathan Davidson-Smyth one to one, and not bring along another solicitor or brief as he had suggested. I had it in my mind that I would listen to what DS said, and then decide on whether or not I needed any advice from another third party. Arriving at the Connaught, I was expecting a larger hotel, especially it being in Mayfair. DS was at the door and directed the doorman to meet me and asked me to follow him to a small space, with a table and a couple of sofas, where DS was sitting checking some papers. He didn't look up straight away and made me wait a short time before greeting me with "good day Mr Holmes, just catching up with some paper work."

"You should delegate, spread your workload, if it's too much" I answered coldly.

This did bring a "Sir" out in his quick reply.

"Mr Graham" was more laid back and let me run things, Sir."

"That's alright" I answered, "I'm just testing the water, now where's that lunch?"

DS caught the eye of the Hotel Manager who seemed to have everything arranged, and guided us into the dining room, "Your table, Sir" and looking at DS said "would you like the menu right away Sir?"

DS looked at me before answering and I nodded my approval. The menus came over and was asked if we would like the wine list, we ordered. We made our minds up as to what we wanted to eat and I sat back quietly and waited for DS to say something. It's a trick I learnt as a reporter, ask people questions and they come back with answers. Keep quiet and they usually tell you what you want to know. DS was of course a lawyer, or he did not know the rules, he just sat still and sampled the wine, so I had to think of another way. "How much did Stuart pay you for your services". I said coldly.

"Would you like to look at the accounts" he answered "I asked you a question, how much"

"£65,000 a year Mr Holmes"

"Could he afford it" I said.

"Yes sir"

"Bottom line, how much did he leave me?"

"Not counting property, £2.5 million"

"How long will it take to clear it" I asked.

"Not very long, Mr Graham knew he was dying and so, we had ways of moving it around, it should be in your account within days Mr Holmes".

"I took the liberty to have an accountancy firm make enquiries in my name and I thank you for allowing them full access, I also had your firm checked out and I would like you to continue working for me. "Did you know he was gay?" I asked.

"Not until he knew he was dying"

"Did he have a long term partner, you know, boyfriend"

"If he did Mr Holmes, he must have been invisible; he had a girlfriend who lived with him for years. I met once or twice each year, we hardly ever exchanged words".

By this time, I'd paid the bill and made our way to the exit into South Audley Street. "This way Mr Holmes, we're just around the corner".

We crossed the road walked up towards Grosvenor Square, first turning on the right, Mount Row, Lime House.

It must have been the wine, because I felt rather dizzy. DS had given me a guided tour around my offices, which was a Grade II listed house turned into offices in the middle of Mayfair. No wonder I felt dizzy, in the last three days I found out I owned a fantastic house in Chigwell, £2.5 million, a house in Mayfair with other properties dotted around the world. I'd read the will a hundred times and could not figure out the bit about bringing more happiness than it had brought Stuart.

DS said he had arranged a board meeting of which I wanted to know more about. "I will give you a list of directors, and if you wish, I will go over each one of them with you before the meeting" he said and reached into a folder and pulled out another folder with my name printed on the front. "I told you we had time to arrange things prior to Mr Stuart's death, even with you having the most shares you had to be voted in, even in your absence. If there is anything you want or need, we'll go into the meeting"?

I had been following him around the house and we had arrived outside two large Mahogany doors, he pushed them open and announced me. There were four men sitting around a large table and as we walked in they all stood up. DS spoke out loudly, "gentlemen, please meet Mr Daniel Holmes, your new chairman". They remained standing as I was led to the head of the table to my chair; DS pulled it away from the table and beckoned me to sit. I sat down and they all sat down after me. DS again took to his feet and addressing the four directors, said he would like to introduce me to them and read out a rather long letter explaining the will, its contents and of course, he then wanted them to introduce themselves. The man sitting on my right stood up.

"My name is Yin Lee, no relation to Bruce, but I can claim to come from the same country as you can see, I have been a faithful servant to the company for 42 years, man and boy, my father went to school, in China with the honourable Mr Chang. I was sent to work in the construction company, learnt the building trade from A to Z. Never dreaming that one day I would become a director. Mr Holmes, you have my 100% loyalty". He then sat down, the next one stood up, he was a large, quite fat china man.

"My name is Ming Doo, I did exactly the same as Mr Lee, the only difference is my life was in food, groceries, exports, it was destined that way, by whom, I know not, but I thank my god every day and my loyalty has no boundaries.

The next one stood up and at once I knew that it was Mr Chang's brother I'd seen him before. " I know Mr Holmes, you must have been 10 years old the last time I saw you, 1958 I remember it well, I left to return to China, Hong Kong and this is the first time that I have been back. I handle the company's accounts, I am a director of the five links, you of course as well as being chairman, are the director of the Limehouse Link, the links have been joined together since 1890, I like all the directors of the links, would die to keep the links in one unbroken chain. I encourage you to join us". The last of the four rose to his feet.

"My name is Mr Wong, it is my duty to point out to you what we are asking you to share with us, you have been made chairman, precisely so you can have the casting vote, if the occasion arose, you have been nominated by the late Mr Stuart, who has left you with a small fortune and 20% of the shares of the Five Links, as a nominated director, you can use your vote if as on this occasion it has arisen, the other directors are divided, two for and two against. I must tell you what you will be voting for or what you will be joining if you vote yourself in. The Five Links are non-political, non-religious and is not a brotherhood of any kind; it is an international company dating back to 1890, spread across five continents, linking them together, the Olympic Games (modern) could have followed our example in 1896. The Link was formed by the Chang family and somehow, with many highs and many more lows, have kept trading over 99 years. It is based on hard work and goodwill. If you vote to stay in there are many rewards, if you choose not to stay, your shares will be passed on to another candidate, and you will be paid the sum of what the shares were, when they were purchased. The same rule applies if any director or the Link he governs strays away from our fair trading policy or breaks the law in any fashion. Because it is based upon simple rules, hardwood and goodwill, you vote will be accepted now, but you can simply walk away at any time and your shares will be passed on to the person of your choice, or leave it to the other link Directors.

Do you need time Mr Holmes, if so just state how long, although one calendar month from today is the allowed limit." Mr Wong sat down.

Davidson-Smyth rose to his feet. "Mr Holmes, how do you vote, could you give us your answer?" He sat down and looking at me, signalled me to rise.

I stood up slowly my head buzzing, everything was happening too fast and I needed a million answers to a million questions of which I knew nothing about.

"Gentlemen, I would like to take my time to answer or use the vote I have been given. The little I know about your organization is that according to what I have heard, most of the people who have made it to the top, you gentlemen, have got there by extremely hard work which seems to make me the odd one out. I am honoured to be in such a position that I find myself in, and take this opportunity to thank everybody concerned and hope if I decide to remain in your organization, I will not let myself or you down ".

Shang Yang stood up.

"We did not reach this position by benevolence and righteousness, but by taking advantage of opportunities that is all that is required, indeed, using the hard work and goodwill of others, together with our own hard work and goodwill, which has been exploited for centuries, indeed your own "Link", Limehouse started as a reversal of drug trafficking and gambling that could be found in China in the 1830s with Britain's triangular trade of tea and silk from India in exchange for Opium. Culminating to the treaty of Nanjing which gave Britain extra territorial rights in Hong Kong. Mr Shang Yang held up 2 sheets of paper. "Most of what I have just said was written by you Mr Holmes, from you columns when you were a reporter 25 years ago. Even after your unfortunate beating concerning your friendship with Meigui Chang, you somewhat defended China's right for the Treaty to end."

"I thank you for that support and salute the British for making Hong Kong what it is today. Again it was maintained by goodwill and lots of hard work. If you vote yourself in, you will have our full support; it is in all our interests, not to have a weak 'link'." Shang Yang sat down.

Davidson-Smyth, after a short time, rose.

"If there is no further business, gentlemen, can I presume that we meet three weeks from today, giving Mr Holmes a chance to ask you, any questions, before giving us an answer. Gentlemen, I close this meeting."

Everyone shaking hands and then bidding each other farewell, until the last one had gone, leaving Davidson-Smyth and myself in the middle of the room. Davidson-Smyth always seemed to have something to attend to. I stood there watching him signing papers and filing them into his heavy suitcase, which he always had. In fact, if he wasn't making speeches, he was filing. I could imagine him in bed with his suitcase on the pillow next to him.

(Here I go again, as soon as I'm under pressure I have to turn everything into a joke.)

"I'm quite worried about taking this job on," I said out loud, "although the challenge appeals to me."

"I will be at your side at all meetings to help, but nobody will ever do anything but help and encourage each other. It is their way."

"Will the fact that I'm not Chinese make any difference?"

"Being non-Chinese has never been a problem to me or staff, which numbers five. One of them, although not Chinese, has a degree in Chinese language, which is of great use to us."

"How did Stuart fit in, or manage?"

Davidson-Smyth was, unlike him, slow to answer, but eventually replied, "Mr Holmes, it is the company's rules not to dwell over the past but to look forward. If any mistakes were made, any wrong doings or misdemeanours did occur, and I stress the word 'if', you well be advised as to the ways the company works," and quickly added, "in answer to your question, Mr Stuart was a very good businessman, but to be quite frank, he lacked compassion and made enemies, with respect, he seemed to have no friends, and was very difficult to communicate with. One could never contact him." Davidson-Smyth added, "I have quite a lot of paperwork to do Mr Holmes." I knew he wanted to get on, so I decided to make my exit and interrupted him, "I have a few things that I want to take care of, when is it a good time to see you? Is there some kind of programme I'm expected to follow?"

"I am forbidden to explain in fine detail until after you use your vote, but the business in general is franchising, supplying, leasing and, of course, storage."

"Would it be a good idea to meet early next week Mr Holmes, to give you some time to settle? Oh, and will you be having a chauffeur?"

"Yes, thank you," I answered, and already he was speaking into the intercom to arrange for a car ASAP.

We shook hands. "Thank you for everything... err..." I hesitated long enough for him to say "Jonathan, Mr Holmes, and good luck."

"Thank you Jonathan," I said, and made my way down this really grand wooden staircase that separated the house into two units.

The car was waiting, and as I came out of the front door and stepped into the street, the driver was ready with the door opened.

"Good afternoon sir, are you Mr Holmes?"

"Yes," I answered.

"Where do you want me to drive you, Sir?"

"Chigwell," I answered, and added, "Do you know where it is?"

"I used to drive for Mr Graham, Sir. Are we going to the same house?"

"Yes," I said. "What's your name?"

"Godfrey, Sir, but my friends call me God."

"Right, Godfrey, are you a safe driver?"

"You're safe in the hands of God, Sir."

In what seemed no time at all we'd gone around Barclay Square, down the back streets, across Regent Street, around Eros, down the Haymarket, past Trafalgar Square, Charing Cross, Strand, then the traffic got bad so "God" did a quick turn-about, shot down a side road, went underneath a building, using the car park, and came out on the Embankment next to the Thames, past Blackfriars Bridge, through to Upper and Lower Thames Street, past the Tower of London. The Highway was busy, so he took a right turn down Wapping High Street, back onto the Highway towards the Limehouse Link, and then to a standstill. God seemed annoyed and said, "Sorry Sir, but before the Limehouse Link you could get home faster."

"Why did they build it then?" I said.

"Just to keep the traffic away from the warehouses which are now £1,000,000 homes for the elite."

"Who keep us all in work," I replied.

"I was not complaining, Sir."

"I know that, God, I think they call it progress."

"We are not making much progress tonight, Sir."

I closed my eyes and sat back thinking I'd made more progress in a week than I had in all my years and my mind wandered back to my childhood days. Me, Graham and Meigui and a thousand different thoughts, and I still didn't find out who the lone ranger was, you know, the guy buried opposite Stuart, the Unknown Warrior". I wonder if political correctness will change that to the Unknown Victim.

"We're here Mr Holmes."

"Thank God," I said smiling to myself. "You sure you haven't another nickname?"

"No, Sir, my mother was a church-goer and she wanted me to be free, so she named me Godfrey."

Oh, I forgot to tell you, Godfrey was a Jamaican. Already I like him; you couldn't help but like him. He seemed not to have a care in the world.

"What do you do now?" I said.

"Clean the car, have rest periods, I really adjust my life to your routine. My orders are to stay around as long as you need me, 24/7, Sir, and I report to Mr Davidson-Smyth in any emergencies."

"How are you paid?"

"I'm on a monthly salary, paid into my bank. It's a very good job, and I hope you want me to continue, Sir."

"How long were you with Stuart Graham?"

"12 years, and loved every minute, Sir. He often spoke about you, Sir. It was a cruel way to die. A terrible thing to do to another human being."

"What are you thinking about, God?"

"I'm sorry Sir, Mr Holmes, it was just something Mr Graham said to me after I drove him to the specialist and he got his results - his bad, bad news."

"Well come on, elucidate, what did he tell you?"

God was struggling; he wished he had never started. But I wouldn't let him off the hook, and then he blurted it all out. He really wanted to get it off his chest. But what he told me could not be proven. At that moment, I decided to vote myself into the company. What God had said indicated that Stuart's death was somewhat suspicious, or was God making it all up or adding a few words to a sentence from Stuart who had just been told he had a short time to live? No, I'd made my decision. I was famous for this. When Danny Holmes thought he was right he'd grab the bull by the horns and rush in, feet first, usually ending up out of work with egg on his face. In no time at all I had decided that somebody in the "Links Corporation" wanted Stuart out of the way. Already I was compiling a list of suspects and it had to have had something to do with the flowers - and that person buried opposite Stewart.

I opened the main door, and as I did a small black cat dashed inside, me-owing as it moved towards the kitchen. God was standing behind me and seeing the cat said, "That's Brandy, Mr Graham's cat. Is it OK if I give him some food, Mr Holmes?"

"Yes, go ahead," and looking about the house, listening at the foot of the stairs added, "Looks as if my lodgers are out, God. Have you met Stewart's half-sisters?"

Many times, Sir," replied God and went quiet.

"Come on God, say what's on your mind."

"Mr Graham told me he had not spoken to them for many years, and when Mr Graham got ill, I told Mr Davidson-Smyth who then contacted the girls".

"Well, Mr Holmes, whey they found out he was, he was going to die, and did not have much time, he also told them he was a top man with the company Links, which they knew nothing about. Then he said it was his decision to choose who was to replace him. They argued against one anotherwho it should be. Mr Graham then decided to give them a business each and said he knew just the right person to appoint. "You, Sir." But made me swear I would not tell a soul". So that's why they were so mad. They wanted it kept in the family. I was thinking to myself now, going over the scene at the Prince Regent, the hostility I felt and the looks of almost anger on faces from the "Chang" family. What I did not know, at that time, is that I had been left all of Stuart's worldly goods, a King's Ransom, that they rightfully thought should go to one of them.

God had by this time fed the cat and was awaiting my next words which were, "Tomorrow's a busy day, God. I've to go to the office, meet my bank manager, go to the gym and in the evening I've got my reunion with a few of the lads from my childhood days. Do you work out?"

"With respect, Mr Holmes, you don't look like this driving behind a wheel all day. I work out three or four times a week."

"Are you married?"

"Yes, I'm married, got two lovely kids, a mortgage, and a lot of unpaid bills, Sir. You must know more about me than Mr Graham knew in the last 12 years, Sir."

"God, I'm sorry if I have somehow offended you, but I'm new to all this, and I'm asking all the wrong questions. What I meant to say was, have you no home to go to?"

"Mr Holmes, there is no need for you to apologise to me. It's just that over the last 12 years Mr Stuart hardly said a word to me, then on his deathbed he confided in me and I swear I did not know he was gay, Sir."

"Let's say no more about it. What time do you usually start?"

"Any time that suits you, Mr Holmes."

"I've to be at the office at nine. How long does it usually take?"

"We'll have to give ourselves 11/2 hours, Sir."

"Right, God, I'll see you at 7.30am."

"Goodnight, Mr Holmes."

"Goodnight, God." I just had to smile. I turned around and Brandy the cat ran past and out of the door. Fine, I thought to myself, a nightcap and then to bed.

CHAPTER 3

A WARNING

The doorbell rang. I was just showering, towelling my head, I reached for the intercom. "Christ, God, you're early, come on in."

I got dressed and went down towards the kitchen, and got the surprise of my life. God had turned into a woman.

"Hello," I said, "You're not God."

"And you're not Father Christmas," she replied, and added, "how'd you like your eggs?"

"With bacon," I said, not letting her get the upper hand.

"Right," she said, "raw eggs and bacon."

"Well cooked and sunny side up," I surrendered. "Who are you?"

"I'm the slave you call a housekeeper," she said and added, whilst still cooking the breakfast, placing the Dailies under my nose, "Have you remembered to change the address with the post office? 'No', I wanted to answer, but she gave me no chance.

"Do you want to change my timetable? I'm here five days a week, half day Saturdays. Have you anything special you'd like me to do?"

"Yes", I said quickly. "Sit down, pour yourself a cup of tea and shut up".

"You've got five minutes for a pep talk," she said, looking at her watch, "and I pass on the tea,"

"Right, your name, how long have you worked here, and why are you so aggressive?"

"Giovanna, approximately 10 years and I can't argue with my husband. He left, so anybody I come into contact with gets grief. Can I get on now, are they still here," she said.

"I haven't had my five minutes yet, and no, they seem to have gone," referring to Meigui, Xiang Ju and Mudan.

"How long have they been here?" I asked Giovanna.

"On and off about 8 weeks. It's trebled my work load."

"I'll arrange a bonus for you," I said.

"Can I get on now? I really have got a lot to do."

The doorbell went and Giovanna went to open it. I heard some mumbling and God walked in.

"Good morning, Mr Holmes", said God and handed me the mail that had been pushed through the letterbox.

"Morning, God, want some coffee?" I said, putting the letters into my suitcase.

But before he could answer, Giovanna said, "I'll do it, otherwise there'll be more on the top," she grumbled.

"Nice to see you having a nice day, Giovanna," said God.

"I wish I had time to drink coffee," said Giovanna, not giving an inch.

"You know what they say," said God.

"No, what's that?" replied Giovanna.

"God makes hard work for idle hands."

"Then make it yourself, God, and clear up after you," she said, smiling as she left the room and then after dropping her guard took it out on the cat.

"And if you don't change your ways, Brandy, you'll finish up on the menu, in a Chinese take-away."

"About time we were on our way, God," and made my way to the door.

God opened the door of the back seat and I jumped in the front passenger seat.

"I feel like it's the first day at school," I said to God. "They won't expect you in this early Sir."

"They won't expect me to have made up my mind to take the job, so they won't expect me in at all. We had just gone around Barclay Square, a small crowd had gathered, watching some Chinese Group of people doing tai chi and as usual when nervous, I tried to joke and heard myself saying, "I think I'll get all my staff doing that every morning God, what do you think?"

"Does that include me Sir? I don't mind but I don't think Giovanna would fancy it."

We arrived at Mount Row.

God opened the passenger door and handed me my briefcase. "Good luck, Mr Holmes. What time will you need me?"

"Thank you God, I'll call you at least 2 hours before you're required."

I pressed the doorbell.

"Good morning Mr Holmes, Davidson-Smyth here. The door's open Sir."

I pushed the door and walked in. There was a long narrow passage with a large marble fire-place, with gothic style faces peering out at you. The floor was all marble and echoed loudly as I walked to the far end which opened up to a large staircase. Davidson-Smyth was at the foot of the stairs and welcomed me to follow him up the stairs. If he was a bit surprised he did not show it.

"Would you like coffee, Sir?" he enquired.

"No thank you, Jonathan, my housekeeper Giovanna force fed me," I lied, again nervous, result to joke.

"She's quite formidable, isn't she Sir, but very good at what she does," and added, "but like every staff member she can be replaced Sir."

"Are you here every morning at this time, Jonathan?"

"Most days, Sir, but you have a good reliable staff here Sir and it keeps running on course, even when I'm away, Sir. It's made up by one solicitor," pointing to himself, "one accountant, Mr Jonas, an auditor, two PAs and of course we have a telephonist who carries out all office duties. They are a good team, Mr Holmes, and I hope your chauffeur is to your liking."

The morning was spent meeting and talking to the staff, and then I had to meet the bank manager. Down I went to the bank and I was shown into a side room (what happened to the personal banking where you sat in the main banking hall discussing your business with a queue of people within earshot of your pleadings for an overdraft).

"Good morning," Mr Holmes, "how can I help you?"

"I'd like to see my balance."

"I have it right here, Sir. Err, my name's Mr George," he held out his hand for me to shake, which I did, and he held my hand whilst talking to me. "Mr Davidson-Smyth opened the account for you Mr Holmes, but we would require you to sign so we can see your signature. Now, Mr Holmes, we have a range of facilities, investing and…" I cut him short.

"I'd like to transfer my account to my existing bank, Mr George. Can you see to it today?"

He went red in the face and said, "Have we offended you in any way, Sir?" He went to go on, but I stopped him short.

"Mr George, it's nothing personal, but less than a year ago your bank refused to do any business with me, they would not advance me £1,000. I walked out to the bank next door and they offered me £5,000 unsecured."

"I'll see to the transfer immediately, Sir, but would like to point out that your money would be safe with us should you think to alter your mind. The fact that our criteria for loans seem somewhat strict is that we take every precaution with what is our other clients' money."

"I thank you Mr George, but when will you guys learn that you have to treat people with respect?"

I left the bank and decided to get home so that I could get ready for a special reunion.

God was ready with the car and I jumped in.

"Where we off to, Mr Holmes?"

"Home first, then to a reunion with some old friends. It might be a late one God, did you have any prearrangement?"

"Thank you, but no, Sir. The rules are you need at least one week's notice", God replied, and off we went towards Barclay Square. I open my suitcase to put my glasses on, because I just remembered to open my mail, and looked through to open the ones that looked unlike a bill, Water rates, electric, someone wanting to loan me money, funny that, they would most likely loan me cash now that I'm loaded, hold on what have we got here, I pulled out a sheet of paper and on it was written in bold letters "IT WOULD BE FOOLISH MR HOLMES TO EVEN CONSIDER BEING THE HEAD OF THE LIMEHOUSE LINK, YOU COULD EVENTUALLY END UP LIKE STUART GRAHAM".

I read the letter three or four times, and looked at the postage mark on the envelope, "Hong Kong" "that's nice of them, they never bothered to sign it", I muttered to myself.

"Did you say something Mr Holmes"? God asked,

"No God, just talking to myself" I replied, but already the doubts were beginning to take effect. Is this what Stuart meant by, "I hope it brings you more luck than me"? I wondered if he was being got at, but I decided to let things take their course, and see what happens. "I'll see you in the morning God, I'll get a taxi"

"Yes Sir Mr Holmes, goodnight sir."

I arrived at the Do about 8 o'clock and was met by a dozen old friends. Nibbo Wilson, Dandruff, Calvey, Terry Farmer and one or two I could not put a name to, but seemed to know me. Their wives were sat down at tables and after meeting the lads at the bar I was taken by Nibbo to meet the girl I knew as Joan who had married Terry Farmer. As I remember him he was muscular with blond curly hair, but had changed dramatically over the years. He was very fat and hardly had any hair. Alfie Coles, the pub landlord, and a mate I'd known since I was in infant school, had laid on a nice spread, welcomed me in, and introduced me to a couple of SPYSs (South Poplar Youth Club) "you remember these two, Danny", "remember them, I've still got their stud marks in my legs, nice of you to come lads". Nibbo came over and said, "won't be long Danny, I've got to see a man about a dog", what's his name", I asked, and added "Borny Boy".

"Christ, you got a good memory Danny, how much did you lose", "a king's ransom", I answered. "Your idea of a king's ransom then was about a tenner" and off he went. Nibbo was always seeing a man about a dog. He would have been a millionaire if he had not been taken to the dogs when he was only a boy. He graduated from walking and exercising the greyhounds to running them for hours on end around Hackney Marshes, which was conveniently placed adjacent to Hackney Wick Dog Stadium. He was always over the Wick. We used to send his birthday cards to Track 1, Hackney Wick. He was there so much we thought he lived there in a kennel, but he got us back, he told us he had a hot tip, a real red-hot tip, Borny Boy. It just can't lose he said and kept on so much that we all, five of us, put in £10.00 each, some of us borrowing the tenner because we did not want to lose out. Of course the bloody thing lost. Nibbo told us it got bulked on the left bend. The following week it ran again. After it lost,

Nibbo made excuses, apparently it did not like beating bitches and there were three in the race.

The following week it was running again (if we can call it running, no bitches, it came in fifth out of six). Nibbo was not giving up, he tried to persuade us to bet on Borny Boy again, but could find no takers, except Stuart. It won by ten lengths. The only good to come out of this was I vowed never to gamble again, although thinking back, Stuart put a fiver on it for me, without telling the others, because he said he knew that I was skint. I'd forgotten the little things that Stuart had done for me, and they began to add up. He hated the thought of me going out with Meigui. I got embarrassed just thinking about the way I would catch him looking at me; he always wanted my company, snapped and sulked over almost any little thing, then turn up as if nothing had happened. Stuart's name came up a few times, but the night seemed to fly past, and I was in a cab on my way home.

The lights were on, so there was one of the girls back. Giovanna won't be happy. I opened the door. Brandy the cat ran from the garden, jumped over my feet. "Where you been, out on the tiles?" I said to the cat.

"And where have you been, a man of your age should have been in bed hours ago."

I'd had a drink so I was bolder than usual.

"Haven't you got a home of your own?" I said.

"Yes, but I thought I'd come over to see if you needed anything," answered Meigui.

It was easy to answer "No" after the week I'd had. I'd been left over £2,000,000 property, shares, plus a chauffeur, housekeeper. Wait a minute, there is something I been short of lately. Meigui read my mind, "Sex is not on the menu."

"Who mentioned sex?"

"You're a man, aren't you? Or are you hiding something?"

"Would you like a coffee?" I said, hoping she'd say yes, because there were answers to a few questions, she might be able to help me with.

"What you mean is you want me to make you some," she said heading for the kitchen. "How's your week been?" She placed a mug of coffee in front of me.

"It takes some beating," I replied.

"Are you going to take the job on?"

"I think I might, but I want to know more about it," and added, "What can you tell me about it?"

"Very little," she replied. "Stuart never let on what he did." And after a thought added, "we were in Hong Kong and China when our father and stepmother died. We were told very little, and neither saw Stuart for a number of years, maybe as long as ten years."

After two hours of rolling back the years, going over good and bad times and a couple of drinks, I was ready for bed. I needed a cuddle. We reached the top of the stairs. Outside the guest room she had commandeered, looking me up and down, she said, "You still can't hide your feelings, your room or mine?"

Next morning. Could things get any better? I doubt it, Meigui was up, I could smell the coffee. I had a quick shower and wrapped the towel around and went down to the kitchen.

"Good morning, gorgeous," I said, entering the kitchen. "You're up early, Meigui, I…"

"You're mistaking me for someone else again, "said Giovanna. "Last time you thought I was God. Do I look Chinese?"

"Hello Giovanna, I thought you…" Giovanna did not let me finish, as usual.

"Never mind that, she's gone, said she'd phone you, left her number, there's some headache tablets, coffee in the pot, do you want breakfast, that cat will be the death of me."

"Giovanna, please stop," I said holding my hands over my ears. "I'll have a coffee but I'll pass on the breakfast." And to lighten things up, I added, "oh, and you're right, we'll have to stop meeting like this," as I pulled the towel tightly around myself and tucked the edge inside. By this time Giovanna had placed the coffee in front of me and was feeling the iron to see if it was hot enough, and started to iron.

"Did you know Stuart was gay, Giovanna?"

"Yes," she answered and added, "He didn't know that I knew." She went on, "his girlfriend let it out of the bag, although I had my suspicions, and she didn't take much prompting. Apparently they had some kind of deal she would act as his girlfriend so nobody would guess he was gay. But there's something else I think you should know."

"What?" I said.

"Helen, Mr Stuart's girlfriend, was seeing somebody else, Lenny, who knew about their arrangement. You know, Helen and Mr Graham. And Lenny was blackmailing Mr Graham. This Lenny came to the house and I heard him threatening Mr Graham."

"Thanks for telling me Giovanna. Stewart didn't have many friends, did he?"

"If he did, Mr Holmes, they never came here to the house whilst I was here."

I got up, put my cup in the sink and spoke to Giovanna. "You work hard, Giovanna, have yourself an early day."

"I'd rather not, Mr Holmes, there's a lot to be done and I've sworn to myself that one day I'll get in front, but it ain't happened yet, the more you do."

As I made myself up the stairs I heard her shout at the cat. I reached my room, lay on my bed and closed my eyes. I wanted to switch off, but since the letter I had received from the solicitors requesting me to attend the funeral of Stuart, things had been moving fast. I'd had no time to catch up.

I must get my act together, put the pieces together, what do I know?

The funeral went off all right but I got that strange feeling that the Lone Ranger, whoever he was, had some connection. That stupid message from your flowers. The chauffeur didn't want to know and seemed afraid to tell me anything, even Meigui cut me off short and has never mentioned anything although to be fair I've never asked. Then at the hotel, after the funeral, the Chinese looked at me with hatred, I can understand that, they'd been cut out of the will.

Now I hear Stuart was being blackmailed and what God told me, relating to Stuart's death, and of course Stuart's last message to me. "Beware of the flowers", we're back to the Lone Ranger again, add the warning letter to all that, I must have a few enemies.

Over the next couple of weeks, Meigui and I met and she finished up sleeping over at the house. I thought that I would let things cool and hope that I could find out more about Stuart's life style and his partners or gay friends. Then one day Giovanna placed my breakfast papers and my mail on the table. After eating my breakfast, I picked up the top envelope, opened it and started to read. "Mr Holmes, we must meet in secret. You don't know me but we met in Hong Kong one night in a bar. You were with your wife and I was with my Stuart. Please call me at the above number." That was all it said. I got dressed, went downstairs and right on time God came to take me to the office. I got into the car and we were on our way.

"Can you go through Chigwell and stop at the paper shop please, God"

"Do you want me to jump out and get you something, Mr Holmes?"

"No, just let me out, I won't be long."

My heart was beating fast, for some reason, call it second sight or whatever, but I had decided not to use the house phone or my mobile. The danger signals were flashing in my head. I pulled the letter out of my pocket and dialled.

A person named Russell answered. I told him who I was. He sounded very distressed and said he was still devastated by Stuart's death. He went on to tell me that he had been with Stuart for many years until they had murdered him, explaining how Stuart had died, which tallied with the same story God had told me, although Russell did know the third person he thought was involved.

I asked him if he knew anything regarding Stuart's last message, "Beware of the flowers", but it didn't ring any bells and he thought Stuart's mind had become somewhat scrambled with the effect of the pills and other treatments. The third person involved was a Chinese man called (wait for it) Willy Wong, who lived in Hong Kong. Russell said that he was well known in most of the gay clubs, near the city centre. I told Russell I'd phone him sometime next week and hung up.

"Don't tell anybody about that phone call God" I had a habit of not trusting anyone and was testing God.

"What phone call Mr Holmes?" God replied, showing me he was on my side. I would have liked more time to get to the truth with how and why, or indeed, if Stuart was murdered but today I was using my vote to join the Links together.

Mr Davidson-Smyth let me in and said he would be up in a minute. As I walked down the hallway to the stairs I glanced back. The main door was opened and Davidson-Smyth was talking to God.

Davidson-Smyth joined me and began to go over any last minute questions, but was interrupted when my mobile phone rang. "Hello, Danny Holmes". It was God.

"Did you say stay local, Mr Holmes," asked God.

"No God, I said I'd call you when I'm ready," I answered, now annoyed because I'm thinking he's checking up to see if my mobile's working, knowing I used the phone booth. God said something else, but I could not hear. "You're breaking up; I'll call you when I'm ready."

Davidson-Smyth looked up, "Having trouble with your mobile Mr Holmes?"

"No," I answered, "just a bad connection."

Was I getting paranoid? Did I sense something sinister about Davidson-Smyth, something I'd not noticed before? I'd better be on my guard.

The meeting with the other Links went off quite formally. They all welcomed me into the fold, with carefully chosen words, but watching their faces around the table whilst they all took turns to offer any help on decision making, (being nervous) I made a mental note never to play poker with these guys. They reminded me of Edward Munch's Scream. But I must say they were very polite and courteous at all times. The basics of the business were that you traded mainly with Chinese. The "Links" traded worldwide and brought very large amounts so they could realistically get items much cheaper. Each link was responsible to get the best prices and keep stocks turning around. The more you turned around and ordered new stock the more control of the producers you gained, the more they relied on you to keep them in business and if the smaller trader buying from you did not work hard enough and came to you for stock, you could pull the plug and put him out of business, mainly due to the fact that many years before we had franchised him with the shop, with accommodation above, balancing and controlling each restaurant, shop or back street gambling dives, which have helped the Links to prosper over one hundred years. The only thing missing, and certainly was not mentioned, was that I expected there to be somebody at the top, pulling the strings, there just had to be maybe the Triads, or Mafia, or even the Masons. Was I about to see the Grand Master? Nobody had given me a funny handshake; I hope they're not planning an initiation for me. My mind was in a whirl.

Had I been too hasty in taking the job on? Did anybody else want it, apart from the girls? I'm just being silly. Stewart held the job for years. He made a lot of money but said he hoped it would bring me more luck than it did him. But then if what God and Russell said is true, that's what he meant by bad luck. And that's what finally made me link up, to find out who killed Stewart. I now think it's more important to find out why he was murdered, if indeed he was murdered.

Word must have got around that I was new in the job and I was being bombarded with requested for more time to pay, rent reviews, changes to leases etc. Not that I had to answer the letters. Davidson-Smyth & Co took care of everything. I just had to sign and say I approved, and with Davidson-Smyth's help I quite enjoyed my daily commuting to Mayfair. Jonathan Davidson-Smyth was a tower of strength, if he had any faults it was he was so quick at thinking he knew what you wanted before you had asked. I suppose he was quite condescending really, always saying things like, what you want to do is, as we've always done is, this or that, and then congratulated me for going along with what he'd suggested, with quirks like, I can see there's not a lot we can teach you Mr Holmes. Anyhow, life was sweet and I did not want to rock the boat and I had plenty of time to make a few calls to a friend, Midge Meldren who was a reporter with Reuters. I arranged to meet him somewhere off the beaten track, near to where God did his keep fit in Wapping. The gym is just off Wapping High Street in Scandrett Street and I told God to drop me off at the Turk's Head Café which was once a pub, now a café with an outside area overlooking the gardens. I told God to pick me up in about two hours.

I ordered a cappuccino and sat down reading the Daily which was always available for customers' use. I'd always felt at home there, even when it was a pub. Me, Stuart and a few of the old hacks would swap stories and usually finish up... "Hello Holmesy. This place has changed. What are you having, G&T?"

"Hello Midge. Been a long time, we had a few good nights in here didn't we."

He sat down and ordered a coffee and another cuppa for me.

"Right, Holmesy, what we got going Danny boy?"

"What I am about to tell you, you will not believe. But I want your word you won't tell anyone unless (I thought I'd be dramatic) something happens to me or I'll give you the whole story, if we can sort it."

I started off by telling him I'd been dragged up just along the road in Limehouse and told him about Stewart, me, Meigui and her family. By the time we'd reached the funeral up the Mount in Chingford Midge had already pencilled the Kray's in as the villains and I hadn't told him how I'd been told Stewart had presumably been killed.

"I'll soon find out who the Lone Ranger is," said Midge. "I'll bet he was one of the firms." He added, "What happens next?"

"You better have another strong coffee," I said. "You'll need it". Midge clicked his fingers to the waitress who, good for her, totally ignored him. I ordered two more nicely; Midge was champing at the bit. "Come on, what happened next?" I'm trying to find the words to describe the look on his face when I told him I'd been left £2,500,000, a mansion in Chigwell, 4 factory units, an office in Mayfair. I told him about Charley "Chang's" Angels wanting me in a foursome and Meigui lusting over my body. I'd adopted a cat named Brandy, we fed him on turkey, he doesn't like fish, plus a housekeeper who couldn't stop talking and a chauffeur named God who came from West Indies and didn't like reggae music.

"How do you know he didn't like it?"

"We tried him on fish a hundred times; he just would not eat it."

"No, not the cat.The chauffeur."

"I never asked him why, what's the matter?"

"It don't really I suppose"

It went quiet for some time. Midge, so much unlike him, was quiet and did not know what to say. After a while he said, "Are you seeing a doctor. Do you need help?"

"No," I said. "I don't need help, well not from a doctor. I need you to do something that you're good at, snooping, I need some answers," adding, "no, and by the way, when I was going through a bad patch, you came up with £500.00. You've never pressured me for it, its payback time." With that I pulled out my chequebook and simply wrote him a cheque for £10,000. I signed and dated it and pushed it across the table towards him.

"What's the name of that doctor who's treating you?" he said.

"There is no doctor. I'm perfectly sane, what I have told you so far is all true, but there's more."

"I know, don't tell me, they asked you to play centre forward for Spurs and if I tried to cash that cheque it would bounce higher than you could kick the ball, right over Wembley Stadium."

At that moment, God poked his head around the door. "Mr Holmes,

I'm sorry to trouble you Sir, but the doctors will be closed and you asked me to remind you about getting a prescription."

Midge started to look scared. "You had me going then Danny, but go with the driver and I promise to come to visit you" and with that picked the cheque up and tucked it in my top pocket.

Because I did not want God to know too much I said to Midge, "Nice to see you mate, we'll bump into each other again, I hope" and Midge" was gone.

"Sorry to keep you waiting, God. Will we have time to get to the surgery?"

"I think so Sir. Depends on the traffic".

"I haven't seen that guy for 7- 8 years, in there, when it was a pub and then by chance you sit down at the next table." Being a reporter I found it easy to lie, but I felt it was better to let nobody know that I was trying to sort out why Stuart died, was murdered or call it what you want. I must phone Midge and tell him not to go to the police.

We arrived at the doctors. I went in, saw the receptionist and came out with my prescription. The chemist was just along the road so I decided to tell God to go home. "God, I'm going to the chemists and then calling in at The George Pub so I'll see you in the morning."

"Goodnight Mr Holmes," and off he sped. After collecting my tablets, I came out and went into the phone booth and rang Midge Meldren.

"Hello again, Midge, Danny Holmes."

"You all right Danny?"

"Of course I'm all right, what can I do to convince you I'm not a raving lunatic?"

"I don't know Danny, what?"

I thought for a moment and then said, "Right Midge, it's easy. Get into the House Registry System and find out where I live. All you need is my name." Then added, "When you see how much my house is valued at you'll know I'm not lying. Phone me back."

"Righto Danny, you're on."

It took Midge two hours the following morning, when the offices were open, to blag the answers he was looking for and he rang me.

"Danny, about that cheque you gave me."

"What is it, a reunion? Some of the old mob? Yes I'll be there, about eight on Thursday. See you then."

Midge caught on that I could not answer questions. I made the reunion rubbish up because Davidson-Smyth had been going over the books, bringing me up to date as he called it, when Midge rang.

We had arranged to meet at the Half Moon public house in Leadenhall Street Market and bang on time. It was a typical old London pub, very small, very smoky, and very well used, usually by the same faces year in and year out.

"Got you one in, Danny, you're still G & T aren't you?"

"Yes," I answered and added, "Old dogs and all that," handing him the cheque. "Thanks for helping me out when I needed it, Midge. Take the rest as a bonus."

"Let me earn it, Danny. Tell me the whole of your story, I really thought you'd finally cracked up when you told me a guy's given you £2,500,000, eh, wait on, you haven't gone the other way have you, you're not batting for the other side?"

"No, Midge, I haven't. The bit I've not told you are that Stuart was responsible for the death of his stepfather, going back 20 odd years. He claims was an accident, but left the scene and I was his alibi. I told the police he was with me only Stuart, me and now you know this. That's why he left me everything. So what I want to know is one, why did Willy Wong do what he did?"

"Who's Willy Wong?" After I had told him what Willy Wong had done, Midge said, "I'd like to nail that rat. Where's his last address?"

"The Cemetery. He's dead," I replied and added, "I got the district where he lived and the names of the gay clubs he used to frequent. Let me have any expenses, I'd rather you did all the footwork yourself. The less people involved the better."

"I was going to do it all by phone but I'll have a holiday at your expense if you don't mind."

"Take the wife or girlfriend if you like. I'll cover it." It was good to be able to 'splash the cash' for once in my life. I was, for the first time in my life, earning more money than I was spending. We finished out drinks, ordered some more, laughed about old times, before it was time to go home. "Well, see you Danny Holmes; it couldn't happen to a nicer guy. Why'd they call that geezer Willy?"

"If he'd had a large nose they would have called him Nosey Wong," I laughed out loudly.

"Oh I see," said Midge, but I doubt if he did. He was drink than he drunk he was, I think because I had one or two too many. He was one of those guys who could hail a cab quicker than anyone else and true to form he held his hand up and a taxi arrived. "See you Danny," he closed the door and he was gone. "Midge, Midge, there is one thing more I have to tell you" but he was gone, and I had not told him about the warning letter from Hong Kong.

I felt very alone in the city, my city, where I'd grown up a couple of miles away. I had all this money, properties and all the rest but I didn't feel good. In fact, I felt bad. I was walking along trying to find a cab and bumped into somebody. They were Chinese. I mumbled "Sorry" and walked on down towards the Monument Station. Was I imagining it, but London was full of Chinese. I could not find a taxi anywhere so I decided to go by train. I was really feeling bad, I had drunk more gin and tonics than I could take, and my head was spinning. I was delirious, then this big red dragon came out of the tunnel and I swear it was coming for me, so I flattened myself against the side of the tunnel and must have passed out.

The room was all white. I awakened to a lovely summer's day. I closed my eyes against the sun rays, and then opened them and had the shock of my life. The face of a Chinese woman no more than 8 inches from my face was staring down at me.

"Let me out of here," I cried, and she put her hands on my shoulders.

"It's all right Mr Holmes; you hit your head when you fell, at the tube station. I think you must have had too much to drink. The doctor will be here shortly." I sat up and looked around. I was in a side ward in Bart's hospital.

The past few weeks had caught up with me. The pressure I had put myself through, the endless nights I laid awake, planning my next move, not knowing what might happen if the police found out about Stuart's death. Would they discover why he was murdered, would they put two and two together and think I had something to do with Mr Chang's death, seeing that I have done very nicely and I couldn't give them a good reason why Stuart had left me everything. I have all that money and wealth I never dreamed of, but I don't feel secure. I'm getting old, got no wife, family, kids, nobody. If I was to die tomorrow who would I leave it all to? Brandy the cat? No, cut it out, stop being so paranoid. Let's start putting life back in perspective. Let's start delegating, getting things to go my way, positive thinking.

"Mr Holmes, Mr Holmes, are you all right, do you need something?" It was the doctor. I opened my eyes. "No, no, I'm feeling fine, I think."

"You were asking for Brandy. Don't you think you had enough last night?" the doctor said.

"No, no, I never drink brandy, I must have been calling the cat, and his name is Brandy."

"A likely story, Mr Holmes, I suggest you leave the drink alone and make sure you see your GP. Get a check-up, there's a form to sign, the nurse will show you, and don't forget the drink will kill you," and off he went. The nurse came in and told me to sign a form and then to get dressed and I could go.

I phoned God. "God, where are you?"

"I'm outside your house at Chigwell, Mr Holmes." I looked at my watch. 9.35am.

"Come to the café at Wapping. I'll have some breakfast. See you there at 11.15."

"Right to Mr Holmes."

I then phoned the office. "Jonathan, do you need me today? I'm under the weather."

"No, Mr Holmes. If there's anything that needs your approval or signature we could get your chauffeur to fetch and carry, Sir. If that suits you."

"I'll call you later and let you know if I'm all right for tomorrow."

"Thank you Mr Holmes. I look forward to your call," and rang off.

I'd decided to call Midge to find out his program, flights and I wanted to see if he remembered anything from the night before.

"Hi Danny, glad you phoned, did you get home all right last night?"

"You won't believe it."

"I'll believe anything you say if the cheque doesn't bounce."

"It's all legit. Anyhow, about last night, I finished up in Bart's after falling over and bumping my head."

It all went quiet. "You're serious aren't you? I can't work it out. For years you are the straightest guy in the world apart from the few nights we spent on the wet-stuff, and when you rowed with Cathy. Nothing ever happened to you, in fact you were boring."

"You're right, Midge, it's all happening too fast. Do you and Beth still see Cathy?"

"Beth does, of course, they still work together. We're seeing her tonight. She comes to us every Friday. How about meeting up?"

"Have you told Beth about my money?"

"Danny you had my word I would not tell a soul."

"Sorry, Midge, if I can't trust you I wouldn't have confided in you, and Beth was included."

"No, to tell the truth, I was trying to find out a way to spring a holiday on her without telling her where the money came from," Midge said.

"Midge, if you need anything let me know and it's yours. Call it a loan if you want, pay me back a fiver a week. But Midge, don't let the money part spoil our friendship. And I'd love to come to dinner, there's nothing I'd like more. And Midge, just the thought of seeing Cathy," I couldn't find the words.

Midge broke in and said, "I'll see you tonight then."

"Midge, Midge, where?" I asked before he hung up.

"At my place Danny." He gave me his address and hung up. I wanted to tell him about the warning letter, but it was too late he had rang off.

I was just about to put my new suit jacket on when somebody shouted, "I'm coming in ready or not." The door to my bedroom burst open and in rushed Meigui. "I got a dirty video and I ordered pizza," she said and then saw the new suit, polished shoes.

"You've never polished your shoes for me Danny, she's back isn't she."

"Not exactly," I said.

"What do you mean?"

"I'm going to dinner with friends, and yes, she will be there, but she doesn't know I'm coming."

"Oh, how touching," and then she added, "Do you still love her?"

"I don't know. She might see me and take off," I said.

"She'll take something off if she knows you've got a lot of money."

"I'm hoping she will without knowing anything about the money," I hit back. "I'm sorry; I should not have said that, I think it was over between us years ago."

"What about us?" said Meigui.

"It's all too early to know," I said, and added, "Everything is happening too fast. I'm not sure if I can cope. I'm not sure if I want to. If I'd known you were coming…"

She stopped me short. "You would have baked a cake. No it's all right. You go and play happy reunions, I'll take my video and cancel the pizza. I'll phone you," she said and off she went.

I must admit I felt guilty. Throughout my life I'd never messed people around, I made a mental note to not start now, and I never knew how the night would end. I felt excited meeting Cathy again, I'd really missed her, we had gone through a bad time, mainly due to me losing my job, I suppose I'd gone through a mid-life crisis, I was skint, out of work, and I took it out on Cathy. I could not give her the life she deserved, she was working, keeping us afloat, and I resented it. So I left without an explanation, I just cleared out and here I was outside Midge (Steven) Meldren's flat, afraid to knock on the door. I stood there for quite a time and decided I could not do it. I turned away.

"Hello Danny. I guess we've been set up." It was Cathy.

"Hello Cathy. No, I knew you were coming. In fact, I thought you were already inside."

"But you were walking away, Danny."

"Yes, I think they call it no guts," I stammered. "Midge set it up without Beth knowing. As soon as I got to the door I knew it wasn't right so I was leaving."

"Well, there's no way I'm going in. I don't know how you both thought it was a good idea," and with that she walked away.

"Cathy, please don't go. Let's talk. Can we go for a drink?"

"Have we got anything to talk about?"

"I don't deserve it but I'd like a chance to say I'm sorry."

"You're right, you don't deserve it and you've said you are sorry. But this isn't all about you. I want to know why you walked away. I've been waiting years to find out why. And it better be good or I'll… so help me, I'll deck you."

"It's quite simple really," I said. "You deserved better than what I could give you. I felt I let you down, I was not prepared to let you keep me."

"Couldn't you have phoned me to tell me that? You've had years."

"I was too ashamed to tell you, I had nothing to offer you."

"So why are you here now?"

How do I answer her? What can I say? I can't tell her what I would like to, that I'm rolling in money, so what could I say? "Are you with anybody else?"

"What's that to do with you?"

"I was only asking."

"I did have a partner, but it didn't work. I seem to pick all the losers."

"Would you give a loser another trial?"

"No way. He's married some over poor cow."

"You know I did not mean him"

"Oh, you mean you."

"Yes, me!"

"No."

"Why not?"

"I don't want to keep anyone, I'm getting too old."

"You won't have to keep me. I got…"

"What have you got, a car?"

"No, I got a, eh, yes I have, it's not new but I'm thinking of updating it maybe next year."

"You don't think I care about material things do you. If I did I would never have stayed with you in the first instance. Anyhow I know you're loaded and it doesn't change a thing."

"I told Midge not to let on to anybody."

"Hold your breath, it was not Midge. I got a phone call."

"Was it Meigui?" I said.

"No, it was a man, it wounded like a West Indian. He didn't say much except that you're in some kind of trouble, also that your friend had died and left you a lot of money."

"Did he know that I was coming to see you tonight?" I asked.

"Yes he did. That's why I waited for you to go…first I saw you at the door. What trouble are you in, Danny?"

"It's the first I've heard of it. Come for a drink and I'll tell you what happened."

Cathy agreed to come for a drink. We decided to let Midge and Beth know we were not coming to dinner and went into a local pub.

After a slow start and a couple of drinks and me asking all about Cathy, you know, the usual things, how's your job, do you see so and so, how's Beth? Some bad news, her mum and dad, old Todd, had died, some "You should have got in touch with me to pay my respects." Cathy said, "Enough of me, what's going on?"

I went through the whole story, the flowers, lone ranger, Stuart's will, the Links, right up until I turned around at Midge's door. The only thing I missed telling her about was the warning letter from Hong Kong.

"And now you're in some kind of danger," said Cathy. "And you think it was your chauffeur who phoned me. He wouldn't do that without disguising his voice, would he?" Cathy asked.

"How'd he get your number?" I asked.

"It's in the phone book, has been for years."

The night seemed to fly past, the landlord was kicking us out. Before I could ask her if I could take her home, Cathy said, "Get me a cab please Danny, and let me have some time to get my head around all this stuff. Have you got a pen?" And taking the pen she gave me her number. "Phone me, Danny. Give me some time, but phone me." And added, "Be careful". The cab pulled up, she jumped in, said, "see you soon," and was gone.

I was now setting new records. It was four months since I'd had a letter from the bank manager telling me I was overdrawn. I never even managed two months. It's funny, there's nothing I need to spend my money on. I was seeing a lot of Cathy, I wanted her to pack up her job and move in with me, but she turned the tables on me and said she did not want me to keep her. I was her way of saying, give it time, and see if I felt the same in six months.

Midge and Beth were due back from Hong Kong after finding out that Willy Wong had died. Of course we had suspected that he would be dead. Midge said he had found out something else and would phone me as soon as he could confirm it which he had not succeeded in doing when we last spoke.

47

It suited the situation, Cathy not moving in with me. This way nobody knew what was going on, if, in fact, anybody cared. But I decided to play it safe. It was quite natural for me to meet up with an old flame and good friends Midge and Beth, whom I'd known for years, so I did not hide it. I even got God to drop me off at Midge's place, just as Cathy came along, so I introduced God to her so she could hear God speak. After God drove off I said to Cathy, "Was that the voice on the phone?"

"No, not a bit like it. But I'll know if ever I hear it again," Cathy answered.

Midge was at the door as Cathy and I left God. He took our coats and we met Beth coming out of the kitchen.

"Hi Beth, need any help?"

"Grab the side plates, Cath. You Danny, make yourself useful and open the wine."

"I'm a guest," I said.

"You'll be a guest with a thick lip if you don't do the wine,"

"Does she boss you about like that Midge?" I said to Midge. "I just love a dominant woman." He replied. And the girls started to hand the dishes through the serving hatch. We sat down and I made an attack on the roast potatoes.

"Beth, you might be bossy but you make a lovely roast potato," I said and Beth always had an answer.

"I'll roast you if you leave anything."

"Come on, then, tell us about Hong Kong," I said.

Midge told us he'd snooped around a bit and made contact with a fellow reporter from Reuters who was gay and actually knew Willy Wong, and confirmed the rumours were correct.

"What rumours?" said Cathy.

"Why they call him Willy Wong. Somebody draw her a picture," Midge had centre stage and excitedly said, "Can I proceed?"

"Go on," said Cathy. "I hope there's more. You didn't go all the way to Hong Kong to find out about Wong's Willy. Was he famous?"

"Do you want me to proceed?" said Midge. "And no, I did not go all the way to Hong Kong to find out about Willy's Wong, now stop interfering and let me continue. My contact is going to get hold of Wong's."

Cathy interrupted. "You said he was dead."

"He is dead," said Midge. "My contact is sending Wong's death certificate."

"Oh," said Cathy, "I thought he was going to send something else."

"There's a sinister ending to this story. When Willy died, all his family became rich overnight. Some benefactor (unknown) gave them the equivalent to £500,000, which in China is a king's ransom, or in their case, an emperor's ransom. So what have we got Danny?"

"I cannot figure it out. There must be a connection somewhere. We will have to see what the death certificate says and match them up," I said and added, "Did Willy have a job or something?"

"According to my source, he had a one man and his van parcel delivery service to the rag trade." Midge's mate had been busy. "Did he have an office, I'm thinking of files, who he did business with, that sort of stuff".

"Danny, he said that he'd send over a few things he had come across," Midge said, and added, "I was already in the departure area, ready to board when he phoned, so it should be arriving tomorrow or day after."

"Who do you think killed Stuart?" Beth asked.

"We've been told that Willy Wong became a lover to Stuart, and knowingly infected Stuart with his terminal illness, something like AIDS but much worse. What we don't know is why. His death certificate will tell us for sure, if they both died from the same virus, or whatever they call it," said Midge.

"I'm hoping to find evidence that he was diagnosed and fully knew he could give the disease to another before he went with Stuart. All we have so far is hearsay from God and Russell. Anything to add to that Midge?"

"Yes, Danny. It might be possible to get our hands on Willy's, don't interrupt Cathy, on Willy's medical history for a fee."

"You're not saying a lot, Beth."

"No, but I'm thinking a lot," she answered

"Well, come on Beth, out with it," I said.

"I'm wondering whether you should forget it, leave it alone and get back into being a reporter, which you obviously miss."

The silence was deafening. Then Beth spoke again. "Anyone for coffee? Come on Cathy, give me a hand." The girls left the room.

"Sorry, Danny, that was out of the blue," Midge said.

"That's alright, Midge. Beth's most likely right. A woman's intuition and all that."

Beth came into the room, Cathy behind her. She came over to me and hugged me tight.

"Eh, let me go, I'm about to ask another girl to marry me. Ouch, that slipped out. That fraud has a lot to answer to."

"I'm sorry for what I said, Danny, but I'm scared. You don't know what you're getting into," Beth said, releasing me.

"I've known Cathy for years," I laughed out.

"Not Cathy, the Chinese business," she said.

"Have I got any say in all this?" Cathy shouted.

All three of them shouted, "Yes."

And I could see the girls' minds engage into the wedding mode, and I heard Beth say, "where do we begin?" "Start at the honeymoon and work backwards," said Cathy, "and we're not going to Hong Kong." Funny creatures, women. That'll keep them happy whilst Midge and me can find out who done it.

"Are you really getting married, Danny?" Midge asked.

"I suppose I am. Didn't give it a thought until I said it," I lied!

The following day I walked into the office "Congratulations, Mr Holmes," said Jonathan Davidson-Smyth, as soon as I told him the news.

"Thanks Jonathan, you'll come to the wedding, won't you?"

"When is it, Mr Holmes?"

"I've not been told yet," I answered. "There is a half yearly board meeting due next month third Thursday, 28th, and it is in Hong Kong this time. I'll let Cathy know, just in case."

Over the last couple of months, I'd been rather busy. Not, I must say, with the Links Company Business, but was making slow progress on the "who had done it" front. I'd just found out stuff that we had not expected. It turns out that Willy Wong and Russell were partners until Stuart decided that he could give Willy more, pardon the expression, we are talking money here and to add to that, Willy's mum and sisters worked in the lingerie business run by Xiang Ju, Stuart's half-sister. Remember, we found out that when Willy died, they suddenly became rich, when I phoned Russell I asked him if he knew, first about Willy's family and second, who Xiang Ju was. He said he found out since we last spoke, but I never told him that they received a lot of money from someone. I decided there and then he knew more than he was telling.

Also in the pile of papers belonging to the late Willy Wong I noticed a picture of a stunning girl, dressed only in a chiffon nightdress hemmed in lovely Chantilly lace. Titled Xiang Ju, underneath were some flowers – chrysanthemums.

Xiang Ju means chrysanthemum in Chinese. "Gotcha," I thought to myself, and couldn't wait to let Midge know. But I found out later he was going down another avenue, he was finding out that Jonathan Davidson-Smyth had returned a letter to Willy Wong, attached to a photocopied bill from Mudan, with a picture of a girl in a dress, named Mudan, looking as fresh as peony, right there in black and white, the flower story. They could not wait to tell each other that they had been the one who uncovered the culprit.

"Midge, Midge, I've cracked it. I know who paid him."

"No you don't. I found the flower, it was Mudan, or rather peony," he said smugly, "and he was a courier for her, and there's more. Willy's brother worked for her, my source."

"Hang on Midge," I butted in, "Xiang Ju in English is chrysanthemum," Willy's mum and sisters worked for her. They were in it, the whole Wong family, and the two sisters were in it up to their necks."

"Danny, a letter along with a receipt with a picture of Mudan, or peonies, was sent by Davidson-Smyth, I thought that he would have something to do with it."

"I remember you saying it was the Kray's," I said.

"It seems there's a lot of people wanted Stuart out of the way," Midge replied.

"You're right Midge. Motive?"

"Power?" Midge suggested.

"I can give you three more: jealousy, blackmail, revenge," and wrote all four words in my notebook.

"Power is usually the main cause for murdering. If we can establish if Willy Wong knew before he passed it on to Stewart, if he got paid for doing it, main suspects are Mudan and Xiang Ju equals flowers, and Stuart's last warning to you 'Beware of the flowers'. With Davidson-Smyth putting up the money, maybe because he was caught fiddling by Stuart. I think I really cracked it, Danny."

"Let's sleep on it and I'll see you tomorrow night."

"Alright, see you later Danny."

We decided on an October wedding. I say we, that's not quite true. It was decided 50 odd years ago. You see, Cathy's granny was married in October. Her granny had decided that October was the month when there was not much happening, an in-between month, your holidays are over and nothing much is going on until Christmas. A woman's logic. Anyhow, that meant it did not clash with the half yearly AGM in Hong Kong. Of course, if her granny had been married in June, we would have to wait a whole year.

So here I was in Hong Kong with Cathy shopping, in fact buying a present for Beth. Apparently Beth collected handbags. I bet if you looked she was like most women. They collect most things - shoes, suits, perfume, the list goes on. Anyhow, into this store we go, wallet at the ready, and the first leather handbag we picked up had a small red rose in the corner of the flap pocket with a Chinese sign underneath and a large photograph of a lady, bag over her shoulder and named across the bottom Meigui, or rose.

"I don't believe it," I said to Cathy, and added, "I must phone Midge."

"What now? It's 3am over there."

I was already dialling. "Hello Midge, yes I know the time, I'm sorry but I must tell you. Meigui, her name is also a flower. She's a rose, that's it. They are all in it. Beware of the flowers. We now know who the flowers are; we can eliminate the lone ranger, and concentrate on why. I'll let you back to sleep, apologise to Beth, talk to you tomorrow."

"This has got hold of you, Danny. Please leave it alone. You could be in danger, and it won't bring Stewart back."

"I know Cath. Funny thing is, although we were always together as kids, I don't think I really liked him. Nobody did. I mean, we didn't know that he was gay. I don't know if he did, although we didn't call it gay then. I can even remember Stuart making fun of a kid and calling him queer."

"Why did you never tell me, you know, when you met him here in Hong Kong in that gay bar?"

"He begged me not to tell a soul, and I didn't."

"Where is this all going, Danny?"

"I wish that I knew. I asked Meigui what Stuart meant, concerning 'flowers'. I remember her answer. She just said, 'where did that come from?' and no more was said. Talking about Meigui, I told her we were getting married, and invited her to the wedding. Is that OK?"

"Can I bring some of my ex-lovers?" she teased.

"How many?" I asked (fraud again,) I ask for trouble!

"That would be telling you too much," - "Ouch".

I was going to answer, but the hole I had dug myself was deep enough.

I wish I could tell Cathy where it was all going to end. The more I find out, the more difficult everything gets. Elimination is my best bet, or is it? Out goes the lone ranger, out goes Willy. They're both dead. Nothing to gain, but revenge. Why would the flowers, Stuart's half-sisters, want Stuart out of the way? They all knew Willy Wong, even Jonathan. Ah, Jonathan, he told me Stuart's last message to me, 'Beware of the flowers'. He made a point of telling me he did not know what Stuart meant. I'll test him to see if he knows the girls' names are flowers - rose, chrysanthemum and peony, but I'll have to wait for the opportunity to ask him. And then the second letter of warning came through the post, telling me that I still had time to back out.

The happy hour was a scream, if you see what I mean. Jonathan was his busy little self, pulling forms out of his portfolio like a magician pulling flowers - oh, forget flowers - not the right time. Like a magician pulling rabbits out of his hat. "I got a few forms I would like you to read, sign, and send me, eh. Gentlemen, as you know, each Link holder takes the chair on a half-yearly term. This term is the Hong Kong's Link, and the chair holds the final vote out of five, should any voting of any decision stand at 2 for and 2 against." I wonder how they would vote on human rights - don't go there.

The meeting seemed to last for hours. I pictured myself looking like this lot after years in this business, but I must point out that even in descent they were courteous, and I could take lessons from each one of them on not wasting words. Now I was in, it was explained that on entering a link-up, I would link it together with the other links to form a perfect chain. I must explain that I was presented with a solid gold link, after the link-up we unlinked, or de-linked, I was not quite sure which, but I put my link into my briefcase, had a few words with Davidson-Smyth. Not the conversation

53

about flowers which I was dying for - no, not dying - eagerly awaiting to ask him, and stepped out for some fresh air, leaving Davidson-Smyth, who was rushing back to England, time to catch his flight. He was so hard working I decided to get a few gifts back for him and his wife, whom I've not even met. So I arrange to take Cathy shopping. What I decided to buy was any item with the three sisters' logos and names on to give Davidson-Smyth, to see his reaction.

Good idea Danny Holmes. You've not lost your touch, I thought to myself. But I must admit that the warning letters was giving me sleepless nights, I have got to tell Midge just in case something happens. Don't be stupid, nothing going to happen, I was talking to myself again.

We, Cathy and I, had arranged to meet with Midge and Beth on Saturday evening after getting back from Hong Kong on Friday. Cathy and I were still not actually living together, so I got God, who had picked us up at the airport, to take her home after dropping me off in Chigwell. God had just pulled out of the drive, I waved goodbye to Cathy, and turned towards the door, and it opened. It was Giovanna.

"Hi, Giovanna. You're working late."

"Yes, Mr Holmes. I've left you a note explaining that I will not be working tomorrow, but I stayed late today. Is that alright?"

"Of course it is Giovanna. Is everything alright?"

"Well, will you still need me, now you're getting married?"

"I rely on you so much Giovanna, of course we'll need you," I replied, and added, "and we want to see you at the wedding. And before you ask, you can bring a toy boy with you."

"Do you mean that, Mr Holmes?"

"What, about the toy boy? Yes," I said.

"No, not the toy boy, me. You want me to come to your wedding?"

"Yes, and get yourself an escort to bring you."

"I'm back with my husband. Is it alright to bring him?"

"Of course it is Giovanna." And I added, "I knew there was something different about you. You've mellowed, you haven't told me off for a week. How long has he been back?"

"A few weeks," she answered meekly.

"Cathy's taking me back, Giovanna, so we're all in the same boat."

"Let's hope it's not the Titanic, Mr Holmes."

"Que sera sera. What's he doing for a living?" I asked, just to keep the conversation going.

"He works for himself. Or should I say, he's self-employed. He's always dreaming up new ways of making us rich. The last idea was a cleaning company, but it cleaned us out," she said with a bit of a shrug on her shoulders and a half-grin on her face, and added, "but I must say, he works hard and tries his best."

"That's all you need, is hard work and good will."

Did I say that? It's that fraud again. I said goodnight to Giovanna and went inside, falling over the cat that had this habit of running in between your feet.

"Brandy, have you go a death wish?" I was now bending down, stroking and speaking to a cat. I caught sight of him a moment too late, before I took a crack on the side of my head. With stars in my eyes I rolled over, just in time to see the back end of my assailant rush through the kitchen and out of the back door.

When I cleared my head, got to my feet, I realised that I was cut. It was a quick diagnosis. You see, I had blood on my hands. (Remember when I'm nervous I try to joke about things). But this was no bloody joke. I don't mind blood, but not when it's mine.

I called the police, and after a short time a police car pulled up outside the door. After showing his badge and asking me if I needed an ambulance, which I refused, he said to his no. 2, who had been looking around the house, "How'd he get in?" and the other half replied, "It was not a break in, Sargent. Well, not in the sense of breaking open a door or smashing a window. There was no sign of any; he must've got in with a key."

The obvious questions followed. How many people hold keys? And, of course, did they take anything? And you won't believe it (neither did Sargent) but I had not looked.

"I don't know why, but I assumed I'd caught him in the act, and he ran off ". It was then that I realised that I'd not looked to see if anything was missing. I then noticed my briefcase was open and I immediately grabbed it and looked inside. The Limehouse Link had been stolen. Solid gold. "That's what he must have hit me on the head with," I said to the head copper.

"What was it he hit you with, Sir?"

"The Limehouse Link," and added, "a chunk of gold in the shape of a link which, unfortunately, is not insured. At least, I don't think it is."

I watched him writing in his notebook, and wondered exactly what he was putting down. He then finished writing and asked me to listen to what he had written down. "I have got here that you're Mr Danny Holmes. This is your house, you arrived home at 18.30, went inside, bent down to talk to the cat, and whilst you were bending down, someone unknown to you came from behind and hit you on the head and ran off. You phoned the police at approximately 18.45. Myself and PC Newman arrived at 18.58. The assailant had fled. There was no evidence of any break in. You then discovered that an object, the Limehouse Link, was missing form your briefcase. Then you claim that your assailant had hit you with 'the Limehouse Link' which is a solid gold circle that links together along with four other gold links to make the perfect chain. You then tell me you think that the Limehouse Link is not insured. Is that correct, Mr Holmes?"

"Yes, Constable, that's exactly what happened."

"I should add to that, Sir, that there are no witnesses to confirm your story."

"That's correct, Constable."

"Is the Limehouse Link, this gold object, yours, Mr Holmes? Do you own it?"

"I hadn't thought about that Constable. I'd better inform somebody."

"Could I have that somebody's name and address, Sir, and a phone number would help us clear this matter up or maybe not, Sir." I gave them what they wanted, and they left, maybe I should have told them about the warning letters and then phoned Jonathan. "Hello, Danny here," and before he answered I told him what had happened.

"Mr Holmes, Sir, are you alright?"

"Yes, Jonathan, I'm OK. But what I want to know is, A, is the link mine, B, is it insured, and, C, can it be replaced?"

"The link is the property of the company. It is insured, not exactly the link itself, but it is covered. The third question I cannot answer, because they were all made from the same vein, which makes them the perfect chain, Sir."

"Do you think the thief knew what he was taking? Do you think that whoever took it will hold us to ransom, Jonathan?"

"Let's wait and see what happens, Mr Holmes. We will maybe know better before Monday, Sir."

Next day I arrived at Cathy's flat, knocked on the door. "I'll just get my coat," she said, then saw the side of my head with the plaster on. "I didn't know you are trying to give up smoking." She thought that was funny. I didn't.

In fact, I was limping, or in other words feeling sorry for myself and had a terrible headache. I answered, "I gave up smoking 12 years ago."

"What happened then?" she said.

I told her what had happened, well nearly, I told her there were three of them, but I saw them off. She didn't believe a word, so I told her the truth and also what Jonathan said, and my thoughts that I might get a phone call.

We hailed a cab and set off to see Midge and Beth. "Now don't forget, no taking the micky out of my misfortune."

"You have my word," she said, sniggering.

We reached their front door and rang the bell. Beth opened the door, took our coats, never glanced at my head at all, and showed us into their lounge. Midge handed me a drink and asked Cathy what she was drinking, and the three of them burst out laughing. After a few minutes I was laughing too. Midge shouted, "You're lucky you got it on the head, it's the hardest part of your body."

He added, "Cathy told us quickly on the phone what had happened, she said you were annoyed, and asked us not to take the mick, and that made it all the more funnier. Especially when I told Beth the two times before when we got into trouble, you finished up with a plaster on the same side of your head."

Beth said, "Sorry Danny, what did he hit you with?"

"Don't ask," I said, "you don't want to know."

"Yes we do, come on," said Midge.

"The Limehouse Link. And before you think I've had a bang on the head, it's a chunk of gold, a link out of chain, the size of a small plate."

After they heard the full story, everyone, including me, became quite thoughtful. At first, not a lot was said, and then everybody was talking at the same time. "Is it anything to do with the phone call?" said Cathy. "Do you think they knew what they were looking for?" Midge said. Of course, being nervous, I made a joke of it all, saying, "You better hurry up and marry me Cathy, before they get me."

Amid the chatter and noise my phone rang and everyone stopped and waited for me to answer. I listened. "If you want your, little gold trinket back man, I want £50,000"

"I don't think it's worth that much, the price of gold's gone down. Oh, and by the way, that's the worst West Indian accent I ever heard."

"The price has gone up," the voice had changed to a London sound. "It's now £150,000. You should have done business with the West Indian."

"It's quite obvious you know what you have stolen, which tells me a lot about you, so let's say "25,000 and it won't be worth me informing the police."

"Make it £35,000 and we've a deal."

"I said £30,000 or nothing, that's my last offer."

"OK, I'll let you know how to exchange. I'll ring you on Monday," and he put the phone down.

"Why don't we go to the police," Cathy said.

"I'll see if he comes up with the goods. If he does, I'll give him the money and we'll go from there."

"You be careful, Danny. You've already been hit once."

"If he had wanted to do more than take the link and go, he could have done it then, when I was nearly knocked out. No, I think I know who he is."

The night passed without much more being said concerning the link. It was getting late, so we decided to call it a day and I invited them to lunch the next day. So Cathy came home with me, to help heal my battered head. After taking a couple of pills to get rid of the pain in my head, my head hit the pillow and I fell asleep, only to be awakened by a phone ringing in the spare room. I got up, rushed into the spare room, and picked up the phone. A Chinese voice, a girl answered. We couldn't understand each other. She rang off. Meigui had left her phone.

Now I don't know about you, but my brain works better in the mornings. I left Cathy asleep upstairs, came down, let Brandy out got myself a cup of coffee. I must have a pencil and paper in my hand, and here we go again. Who did what, to whom?

"Who had a key to the house?" I wrote down each person's name.

Giovanna, Meigui, Xiang Ju, Mudan, how many more? Ah, maybe Stuarts make believe girlfriend, Helen, maybe Jonathan. It just leaves one little blackmailing punk, Lenny, Helen's boyfriend. I wonder if they still have a key. Giovanna said Lenny was blackmailing Stuart. I wonder if Giovanna knows where Helen comes from, or Lenny, the local pond, no doubt.

When Midge and Beth arrived, the girls got together to talk weddings, after deciding that we, the men, could contribute very little help in that department. So we repaired ourselves to the games room and set up the pool table. Midge said, after spinning up. "You kick off, Danny".

I broke the pack and spot went down. "You remember Lenny the blackmailer, Midge. That's our man. I think he know too much about Mr Chang's death, or enough to open up a can of worms, so I'll pay the ransom. What I would like you to do is find out any dirt we have on Lenny". After waiting for Midge to finish his shot I continued, "That is, if you've got the time." I felt quite embarrassed saying that to Midge. "What I'm trying to say, Midge, that's if you want to, I'd be happy if you would stay with this, me, until we solve it. I don't want us to change. I don't want the bloody money to get in the way of our friendship."

"Just shut up and take your shot. And what were you saying? I was concentrating so much I didn't hear a word." He was called Midge, short for Midget. Apparently he took up boxing when he was a nipper and his trainer, a big black man, said to him, "Christ man, you're so small we'll call you Midge. You ain't even big enough to be called a full midget, boy, you're gonna have a tough life. They'll be queuing up to kick sand in your face." But he had grown up a lot since then, and nobody kicks sand in his face. He'd set Beth on them, he is some guy, and a special friend. "Anyhow, you know there's no way I'm not seeing this through. I'm like a dog with a bone. I won't let go. I think you're stuck with me Danny, we'll get the so-and-so." But is the robbery, the link, Stewart's death, Chang's death, Stewart's warning, are they all one item, linked together by one person, is there a Mr Big?

Monday morning arrived, and I was not feeling good. The numbness had worn off, and the pain had finally got through my thick head and was now engaging my brain. I made my way downstairs to get some painkillers. "Morning, Giovanna. Got any painkillers hanging around?"

"In the top right hand drawer," she said, bending down and pulling washing out of the machine. Without looking up, she continued, "I'll call the man to fix it; it always breaks down when you want to use it."

"You wouldn't know it was broken down if you didn't want to use it, "I answered.

"Just like men. Unreliable," she said.

"Does that mean we won't see him on the Titanic?" I said, relating to our last conversation on Friday, just before I got hit on the head. Hello, is that a coincidence? It wasn't her, what did she call him? Or did she not say his name? It's funny he came back, I get clonked, and he's gone again.

"Glad you think it's funny," she snapped back, and looking up, saw me holding my head. "What you been up to? You're too old to go around getting into fights."

"Thanks for your vote of confidence, but you should see the other guy," I lied.

"Never mind him. That's all you're all good for, making false promises and fighting. Now hold still and let me change that plaster. How did it all start? Why didn't you go to the hospital?"

"Giovanna, Giovanna, please don't go on. Be quiet and I 'll tell you all about it."

At that moment the doorbell went, and Giovanna said, "Don't touch anything. I'll be straight back." I heard a man saying something and into the kitchen came Giovanna and two CID chaps.

The older of the two men said, "We're here about the break-in and robbery that occurred on Friday evening, Sir. It's Mr Holmes, isn't it? You were the person, oh yes; you took a whack on the head."

"Excuse me for one minute officer. Giovanna, we'll leave you to get on. Would you follow me, please," and I took them into the games room.

"Nice place you got here, Mr Holmes. What did you say you do?"

"I didn't," I replied, and added, "I was left this lot in a will."

Silence!

"This 'Limehouse Link', Sir. How valuable is it?"

"I don't really know. You'll have to get in touch with a Mr Davidson-Smyth."

"This Davidson what's-his-name. Who is he?"

"He's the attorney. Solicitor of the company who owns the link," I said

"How comes you had it in your possession?" he asked.

"It was given to me on Thursday last week, and I was just bringing it home to put in my safe."

"Do you know the person who stole it?"

"No," I answered.

The routine questioning went on for over half an hour, until his parting words were, "I'd have your locks changed if I were you, Sir. I'll let you know what's happening. Goodbye, Mr Holmes."

"Giovanna, Giovanna," I called, and we met in the hallway. "Giovanna, I'm sorry you heard all that. I was going to tell you when the dust had settled."

"How did they get in?" she asked.

"We think they had a key. The only person I can think of with a key is Helen, Stewart's friend. Is she a local girl? You wouldn't know her surname, by chance?"

"Green. That was her name. I think she came from the same place that I was brought up in."

"Where's that?" I asked.

"St Pauls Way in Bow," she said.

"How did you end up working here in Chigwell?" I asked.

"Me mum moved to Dagenham because she got a job at Ford's, and brought up me and my two sisters on her own. Dad had died earlier, so it was left to her to bring us up."

"You come each day from Dagenham?"

"No, I moved when I got married to my, and apparently everyone else's, Eddie."

"Another Dagenham boy?"

"No, he came from posh Upminster."

"And Lenny the Blackmailer, where did he come from?" I said, now looking at her seriously.

"You think it was him who did it."

"I think it was him who, yes, did it." I said, holding my head.

"Lenny came from Bow, you know, Campbell Road."

"Yes, I know Campbell Road. I'm a Limehouse boy, same as Stewart was. We went to school together. This Lenny, what was his name?"

"Lomax. I went to school with his sister Ruth. Will you tell the police it was him?"

"No. I should do, but I'll deal with it my own way." Already I was planning my next move.

I phoned Midge and told him what I knew, just to go over some ideas. Two heads are better than one, and what we came up with was we decided to phone Nibbo Wilson and asked him if he knew the whereabouts of Lenny Lomax. Nibbo said he would make a few phone calls. He said he's heard of Lenny and thought he knew someone who did know him. "It's pretty serious stuff Nibbo, so keep it quiet," I told him, and put the phone down.

Midge came up with a good idea. He said "Keep your phones engaged all day long. At least until we find the whereabouts of Lomax." Nibbo and Midge were given Meigui's phone number. It was a stroke of luck, she'd left it behind. I bet she thinks she's lost it; anyhow it will come in handy today.

It was about 17.30, or 5.30pm in old money, and Meigui's phone rang. It was Nibbo. "Danny, Lenny Lomax is outside Walthamstow Dog Track, my source tells me he's hanging around a phone box. I'm just getting there now."

We sprang our trap, I kept Nibbo on Meigui's phone and switched my mobile on. Sure enough it was Lomax.

"What's wrong with your phone?" he said, and the phone was snatched out of his hand by one of Nibbo's heavies.

"We have him, Danny."

"Can't you put Nibbo on, "I replied?

"What you want us to do with him, Danny? Use the shock treatment or set him on fire?" he shouted out loud so as Lenny could hear.

"Offer him a £10,000.00 only for 'the link'. Keep threatening him. If he doesn't come up with the goods, we have to use plan B. The trouble is, we have not got a plan B, and by the way, Nibbo, I was held to ransom for £30,000.00 which I was willing to pay."

"Does that mean there's a good drink in it for the boys, Danny?"

"Whatever you can convince him to take, you can split the remainder of the £30,000 any way you want to, but I want the link back."

"Leave it to me, Danny. I'll have that link back by tonight." With that, he rang off.

By 10 o'clock that night, I was holding the Limehouse Link in my hand, and phoning Nibbo to thank him, "Nibbo, Danny here. Thanks a million. I'll settle with you tomorrow. Where can I meet you? Of course, with the cash."

"Anytime you want Danny, there's no hurry," he answered.

I'll see you in Alfie's then. How about lunchtime?"

"Sure thing, Danny. See you then."

I then phoned Jonathan and told him the good news, before getting in touch with Midge.

"You know, Danny, I don't know how we got away with it. It was all too easy," Midge said.

"I'm glad it's all over, Midge."

"Is it all over, Danny? I wonder how much Lenny Lomax knows concerning the link and blackmailing Stewart. And why are you and I worried about what he knows? And before you answer that I am as much concerned at getting a result as you are, in fact more so."

"Beth knows the answer to that, Midge. We are just a sad old couple of hacks who can't stand losing, or rather know that if you dig deep enough there's an answer to everything. Stewart was a friend of mine years ago. Looking back, I don't think I particularly liked him, but someone had him murdered and we want, no need, bloody need to know why, and I don't particularly like the way they did it."

"So where do we go from here? How about back to Lenny?" Midge said.

"To what end?" I said.

"To see if he would like to tell us what he knows," said Midge.

I'm seeing Nibbo tomorrow at lunchtime. Why not come along?"

"Yes, go on then. Where to?" said Midge"

"The Railway, Grove Road. See you there about 12.30."

"Midge Meldren, Alfie Coles." I introduced Midge to Colesy and Nibbo came in. "Glass of lemon water Danny. Alfie knows what I drink."

We got the drinks and found ourselves a table. "Nibbo, the money's in there," I said to him, and handed Nibbo a packet. "How much is in there Danny?" he said.

"What we agreed. £30k" I answered back.

"Make it £20k. I actually gave him £10k and the two heavies £5k each,"

Nibbo said, and pushed the packet to me. "You got me it back, a deal's a deal," I said, pushing the packet back to him.

Nibbo put it in his pocket. "There's something else, Danny. When we were making out to wire him up, he said something I think you'll want to know. We asked him where the link was and just before we made out to switch on, he said 'the Chinese lady paid me to take it, and if I give it to you I'll need at least £15k to make a new start somewhere else.' I thought if he's taken a drop to take it from you, an extra £5k would help him to make himself scarce, and then he told us where the link was."

"Did he say anything else," Midge asked.

"No. As soon as we gave him his cash he scarpered."

"But you can bet our life the pond life will be back for more cash once he's shot that lot in his arm."

"What is he on?" said Midge.

"I don't really know, but I could find out."

"See if any of his friends can find out who approached him, find out who he deals with for his drugs," Midge said, and added, "Sorry Nibbo, didn't mean to give you an order. Danny's asked me to help him. We worked like this together for years, finding out who did what to whom and who's paying who."

It was three weeks to go before our wedding. Beth and Cathy spoke of nothing else. We were going to spend our honeymoon in Ireland. Both Cathy and I were not sun worshippers. We'd always planned to visit some of Cathy's family who lived in Connemara, which is on the west coast of Ireland where there are more sheep than people, and I was told years ago about the little people and the fairy hills where one side of the hill there is cattle and the other side sheep. There was no fence at the top of the hill, but neither the sheep nor cattle would stray to the other side. Now, if you believe in all that, you believe in anything. And what happens next? Made me believes in anything.

Nibbo rang me up and sounded very excited, and could not wait to blurt out that a face he knew visited the same supplier as Lenny Lomax. Guess where, in a Chinese restaurant. I can just imagine, number 36, prawn fried rice, with some coke on a side plate.

"Have you got the address?" I said to Nibbo.

"Yeah, just off the 'Limehouse Link' The Green Goddess."

"He's one of mine," I said. "Thanks Nibbo, that's another one I owe you."

I could not turn the computer on quick enough. "Green Goddess, ah, here it is. Run by, oh no, Mr Wong - coincidence or what? I must ring Midge."

"Midge, Nibbo just rang me with Lenny Lomax's supplier. It only turns out to be one of my restaurants, run by a certain Mr Wong - as in Willy Wong."

"And you want me to find out if they're family. I feel things are coming together Danny. That Nibbo's quite a lad, ain't he. I'll get back to you as soon as I find out anything."

What with my daily work up at Mayfair, getting my wedding suit tailored, Cathy asking everyday if it was alright to buy this or order that, can we invite this person or that person, something borrowed, something blue, must send an invitation to this one, that one, and bingo, the stag had arrived. Well, you could hardly call it a stag night. The youngest one there was Rubber nose and he was 52 and looked much older. Nibbo was up the front ordering his lemon waters, everyone but his wife knew he had an arrangement with the bar staff that when he ordered a lemon water most of the contents in the glass was vodka. We wondered how his wife hadn't realized how he always got half cut on lemon water. His answer was that after two gin and tonics with lemon she didn't know what day it was and that it was her who was drinking lemon water the rest of the night, you couldn't say he had a dry humour. Since I've been back on the block I've never seen him without a glass in his hand. The old gang was in that night, and I do mean old. There was Rubbernose, better known as Cliff Rabinaue, Johnny Walters, or Arthur, he had not changed one bit. We called him Arthur because he never finished a sentence. "Hello Arthur", yes we called him Arthur, and he answered to it, "It's been a long time," I said, holding out my hand for him to shake.

"I think it's," he said, stopping short.

Rubbernose said "You think what, Arthur?"

"It's going to rain."

"What's Arthur on about?" said Nibbo.

"I wish I knew. How's your lot, Rubber?" I asked.

"About as good as Grimm's. What you want Grim?"

"Lager top, Rubber. You sure you're doing the right thing, Danny?" said Grim, real name Jim Parker, called Grim as in Grim Jim, a right miserable b------.

"See the entertainment's arrived," said Nibbo, looking at Grim.

"Someone's nicked me parking spot." It was Hi-Jack, alias Tim Prichard, called Hi-Jack since he became a lorry driver. He had been hijacked 4 times, even the police nick-named him Hi-Jack.

"I wish someone would nick my misses," said Grim.

"So does she," said Rubbernose.

"All the shops would close down if she wasn't about," said Grim.

"You should do what I've done," said Rubbernose.

"I talked the misses into getting a job in Bluewater. She does all her shopping in her lunch hours, and she gets a discount."

"It's like me," said Arthur.

"What's like you?" said Rubbernose.

"I do all mine," Arthur said, or nearly said.

"All your what, give me breath, it's like having a conversation with a budgie," said Rubbernose.

"You can always throw a blanket over it to shut it up," said Hi-Jack.

"You couldn't, Hi-Jack, someone's nicked yours," said Midge.

"I've never had a budgie," said Hi-Jack.

"What's his name?" said Arthur.

"He hasn't got a budgie," said Rubbernose.

"No, him," Arthur was pointing at Midge.

"Sorry lads, this is Midge. Oh, and he hasn't got a budgie," I said.

"Yes, I have," said Midge, "and he speaks three languages."

"What's he say?" said Arthur.

"I don't know, I only speak English, and that's not one of the three he speaks."

"Someone put a blanket over his head. In fact, it's his turn to buy the drinks," said Hi-Jack.

"The drinks are on me lads, and thanks for coming."

"Best of luck, Danny. You'll need it. Getting married was the worst day's work I ever did," said Grim.

"Happy days, Grim," I replied holding my glass up to his, and added, "But haven't you been married three times?"

"Just like me and my budgie," said Midge. "They all spoke a different language."

"They didn't stop nagging," Grim said.

At that moment Dandruff came in. "Hello Danny. My lads are all right, aren't thy, they're my chauffeurs."

"Hiya Dandruff, thanks for coming. Have a drink lads," and waved to Alfie pointing and saying, "give the lads what they want, Alf."

"Come on Danny, here's the mike, they're playing your song," Nibbo said, and shoved the microphone into my hand and pushed me onto the small wooden stage in the corner of the bar.

"I haven't sung for years," I said, but I couldn't pass the chance up, always believing, especially when I'd had a few drinks, that I was Frances Albert, and the music was "New York, New York".

After the first part of the song, Grim shouted out "You want me to help you liven it up, Danny?" But Dandruff, two lads came forward, one each side of me, and formed a threesome chorus line, and singing away the three of us were kicking our legs out in time to the music. We were just coming to the last line, "If you can make it there, you'll make it anywhere, it up to you New York, New York" when in a flash the two lads had stripped off, and as they took off their baseball caps their long blond hair fell out, and I looked down at them. I knew that I had been set up, they were absolutely starkers.

"Blimey," said Arthur. "They've taken all their clothes off. Look, look, they're not blokes, they are women."

"I've known you all my life Arthur, and that's the first time you've finished a sentence," Rubbernose said.

The song finished, the girls grabbed their kit, and rushed off to the ladies to change.

"You should have seen your face, Danny," Nibbo said, and added, "I've got the photos to show Cathy."

"I had no idea, I was really bashing out that song. You could've given me a heart attack."

It was a great night, and Midge dropped me at my house in the early hours of Saturday morning.

"I'll be round at 12 o'clock on the dot. If I don't get you to the church on time, Beth will personally kill me. I'll call you in the morning. Goodnight, Danny."

"Goodnight, Midge. Don't forget to feed your budgie."

"The old jokes are always the best. I'll ring you." And off he went.

CHAPTER 4

THE WEDDING

"Brandy, get off of that ironing or you won't see tomorrow."

"I'll never get used to her arguing with the cat." I was talking to myself again.

"Morning Giovanna. Any black coffee?" I said as I went into the kitchen, and added, "Anyhow, what are you doing here today? You should be getting yourself ready for my wedding."

"I was asked to meet Graham's sisters here at 8 o'clock, Mr Holmes. Have I done something wrong?"

"No, you have not Giovanna, don't worry about them. You're on my payroll, and there you will remain."

The doorbell rang. "I'll answer that, Giovanna. It might be them." And off I went. Nobody fires Giovanna, not ever. Sure enough it was them.

"Now look here girls, Giovanna works for me," I said as stern as I could be.

They all trooped past me, but not before giving me a kiss on the cheek.

Meigui said, "Morning Danny, is Giovanna here yet?" Xiang Ju said, "We have got a surprise for her," and Mudan added, "I just know she'll look gorgeous in these."

"Giovanna," Meigui said, "we have an old Chinese custom that on the wedding day of the man of the house, the house-woman is waited on, and dressed up by the man's family. We consider ourselves as near to Danny as family, so it is our duty, no pleasure, to dress you up for the wedding."

Mudan then spoke. "Being that we are all experts in the clothing or fashion industry, would you give us the honour of dressing you in our fashions?"

Giovanna was gob-smacked. Meigui said, "We have approximately 5 or 6 hours, which is ample time, so please let it be yes."

"You'll need more than 5 hours. You'll need 5 weeks," said Giovanna.

"Is that a yes?" said Xiang Ju.

"What do you think, Mr Holmes?"

"Go for it, Giovanna, and thank you girls. Is it really an old custom?"

"Confucius said, Customs have to begin sometime, why not the present."

It was Meigui speaking.

"Did Confucius say that?" I said.

"He would have, if he'd thought of it first," she replied.

"Will your husband be there, Giovanna?"

"No, Mr Holmes, he still thinks he's too much for one woman, and I ain't sharing him with nobody, so it's goodbye."

"I'm sorry I asked, Giovanna. Now you go and get dressed up and I'll see you at the reception. And thanks again, girls, it's a really nice gesture." And off they went.

The phone rang. It was God.

"Morning Mr Holmes. God here. Is there anything that you have forgotten that I can help you with?"

"Thank you for asking, God, but no, everything's covered. Just make sure we see you there. Oh, and no driving. Get a cab, on me, you do enough driving all the year. See you there, God."

"Thank you, Mr Holmes. Have a lovely day. God be with you and your lovely lady. I mean the almighty God, Mr Holmes."

I put the phone down and it rang again. It was Cathy. "Are you doing anything this afternoon?" she said.

"No, why?" I answered.

"I thought you might want to get married," she said.

"Not today. West Ham at home and I've got a ticket."

"Well, if you decide not to go, I'll see you after the ceremony, because

I'm marrying somebody today. Beth's made her mind up about that, so be there," she said, and added, "and who were the young men who were singing with you on the stage last night? You looked as if you had one over the limit, and the photos made you look overweight."

I thought Nibbo was only joking when he said he'd show Cathy the photos. She must have seen the ones where they had stripped off.

"OK," I said, changing the conversation, "you be there at 3 o'clock and don't keep me waiting."

"I think Beth will get me there at 2 o'clock or sooner," she said.

"Bet you I'll be there before you."

"You'd better be. Bye for now, see you there," and she rang off.

The phone rang again. "What you forgot, darling?" I said.

"Are you alright, Mr Holmes? It's me, Davidson-Smyth, oh, Jonathan."

"Morning Jonathan. The phone's been constantly ringing. I thought you were Cathy ringing back."

"One of our establishments has burnt down, completely raised to the ground, sir."

"Is everybody alright?" I enquired. "Who is it?" and somehow, I already knew the answer.

"It's the Green Goddess, run by Mr Wong. One of our oldest establishments, Mr Holmes. He's been a friend of mine for more years than I want to remember. I'm afraid that Mr Wong died from the fumes, sir."

"I'm very sorry to hear that, Jonathan. Is there anything we can do to help the family?"

"I'm sure the Chinese community will gather around and provide shelter for his wife and two children, Mr Holmes, but I'll pass on your condolences."

"No, don't do that. Tell me where the family are."

"They are staying with friends at, let me see, I put down the address, here it is, 175 Penny Fields, Limehouse. Do you know it, Mr Holmes?"

"Jonathan, it's in my old back yard. I'll drop by and pay my respects. Oh, and thank you for letting me know. I'll see you this afternoon."

At that moment the doorbell rang. It was Midge. "Morning Midge. Here, if I was to tell you that one of our restaurants had burnt down, which one would you bet on?"

"I'll phone a friend. A Mr Wong, he'll know the…"

I cut him off quick. "You can't ask him, Midge, he died in the fire."

"I'd take the money and run, and if I was you, Danny, that's what I think I would do."

"Especially as Cathy doesn't like dressing in black." As usual, when I'm nervous, crack a joke. "Did you meet my friend Grim last night? You sound just like him." Midge saw the funny side of it, and added, "Was he always that happy? He could've made a fortune as a straight man, for a comedy double act."

"What him and Davidson what's-his-name. Here, do something with this collar stud." I was, of course, getting dressed as we were talking, and was having difficulty with the damn collar stud.

"I reckon the other two characters were a better act - Arthur and, what you call him, Rubbernose. Do they practise daily?"

"No, what you see is what you get. You never know what Arthur is on about, he's always three sentences behind and never finishes a sentence. Old Rubbernose, real name Rabinaue, always uses Arthur to get a laugh."

"Anyhow Danny, we'd better hurry or we'll be late, which would mean you get married, but I'll get dumped. And another thing is, I have not written my speech."

I finished getting dressed and joined Midge downstairs. "Well, how do I look?"

"What, out of 10? I'd say about 2 1/2 million," Midge answered and added, "I'd marry you myself."

"It's a funny thing, Midge. I don't feel any different. The money makes no difference, I've never woken up in the morning any way other than I did before. I have not bought a car, house, or anything you think you like to do if you had won the lottery."

"I suppose that's got nothing to do with the fact that you have a beautiful house, and it's not worth buying another car in case Meigui decides to butcher the tyres again, and the fact that you are chauffeured around in a £60,000 Merc, plus you have a directorship in one of the largest companies in the world, how come you don't feel different?"

"I don't know, Midge, I think I'm too old to enjoy it all."

"It might just take a time to get used to it all. Maybe when you're married, which will be in a few hours' time, Cathy will give you that spark that is obviously missing."

The doorbell rang. Midge looked at me and said, "Righto Danny-boy, let's do it. Got the rings?"

I handed him the rings and he put them in his pocket. "You got your best man's speech?" I asked.

"All in my head," said Midge, "and Beth warned me that it had better not be crude, as if I would."

We got into the car which had arrived dead on time, and made our way down towards Bow Road to the Civic Theatre where the registry office was.

"How are we for time?" I asked the driver.

"We'll be there very early, sir. We allowed more time in case the traffic was heavy but there's not a lot on the road today."

"Do you know where Penny Fields, Limehouse is?" I asked.

"Yes, Sir."

"Could you dash around there, I want to see somebody. It will only take 10 minutes."

"Right away, sir. We're nearly there and it's not a lot out of our way."

In no time at all we were in Penny Fields outside the house where the Wong family was staying. I knocked at the door. "Good afternoon, my name is Danny Holmes. I'm here to pay my respects to the Wong family."

I was shown into a room, and the person who had answered the door came back into the room with three people, obviously the Wong family. "Mr Holmes, Yang Wong was my brother. This is his wife and children."

"I was very sad to hear about the accident, and felt I had to come and pay my respects. I did not know your husband, but Mr Davidson-Smyth speaks very well of him, and said he has been with our company for many, many years, and that he is very well respected. Mr Davidson-Smyth will contact you on Monday, and as you know him very well, he will see if he can give you any help. I'm sorry I cannot be there myself on Monday."

At this moment Mr Wong's brother interrupted, "I must apologise, Mr Holmes, for interrupting. We are honoured that you have taken time out on this, your wedding day. The respect you spoke about is very much appreciated and will help our family to rebuild our faith and strengthen our resolve to continue our lives just as my brother would have us do. Please honour us, Mr Holmes, by allowing us to respect you, and thank you very much for coming."

I said goodbye and headed for the car. Midge was getting frustrated.

"Come on Danny. We'd better get a move on." I got in the car, sat back, and felt good about myself.

"I feel like getting married today," I said, and added, "Come on, driver, get me to the church on time."

I was introduced to the Registrar and shown into a large room. Most of our crowd walked in behind and sat down on the seats provided. There was no sign of Cathy. The crowd, made up from friends and family, were getting restless. There were two people, a man and a woman, acting as registrars. The woman stood up, and everyone went quiet. She was just about to speak when the door opened and in came Stewart's three sisters, all looking fabulously dressed, followed by an equally wonderfully dressed woman - a really good looking dame - Giovanna.

"Is that who I think it is?" I said, speaking to God who was standing quite near to me.

"That's not the same Giovanna that tells me off every morning, is it Mr Holmes?"

The cute lady standing by his side broke into the conversation. "I'll be telling you off if you don't introduce me properly, Godfrey."

"Mr Holmes, this is my wife Roberta. I call her Bobby."

"Hello, Bobby. It's good of you to come, Bobby. I hope he didn't drive. I told him to get a taxi."

"I wish you all the luck, Mr Holmes."

"He'll need more than luck." Who else, it was Grim.

"Nice to see you here enjoying yourself, Grim."

"It's not," said Arthur, standing next to Grim.

"What's he on about now?" said Rubbernose.

The lady registrar called for silence. The doors opened and Cathy with Beth a little bit to one side and slightly behind her walked in. Wow, she looked beautiful. The dress looked stunning. As she slowly floated over the floor and came to my side, me like an idiot said, "You didn't get that dress down the Roman Road." Then added quickly, "You look fabulous, good enough to marry."

"Just something I threw on," she said, and Beth chimed in, "And don't you get too near until the photos have been taken."

"I said to Midge, "She's serious, isn't she."

"Deadly," Midge said.

The ceremony came to an end, and the registrar said, "Go on then, you can kiss the bride." I was just about to, and turned to Beth and said, "Is it alright?"

"Only one, but no clinching," she said, trying not to smile. Cathy and I kissed, I turned to Midge who shook my hand and wished me good luck. Beth came and gave me a kiss and said "You'd better look after her, Danny Holmes, or else talk about the Limehouse Link; you'll be the missing link."

"Where did she get that dress designed? Paris? Rome?" I said.

"No," Cathy said, "I actually got it up the Roman Road. I ordered the material off a stall and the rest was done by Meigui, Xiang Ju and Mudan, who designed and made this remarkable garment, bringing their three labels together, which, they say, is going to be sold all around the world and I have the prototype one. And by the way, I invited them to the wedding to accompany some of my ex-boyfriends."

We men are not like that, we don't have to have the last word, well not always, but I replied, "I suppose that means two of them won't have dance partners."

"Well they can share you, because nobody, especially you, is getting near my dress." And laughingly added, "or they will have Beth to answer to."

Whilst this banter was going on, we had been slowly making our way to the outside of the building, where the photographer had set up his equipment, and unfortunately for him Arthur was giving him some tips on how to use it.

I called over Rubbernose. "Get Arthur off of Flash Gordon's back, or we'll be here all night, cutting down our drinking time."

"I'll see what I can do, Danny, and good luck mate. It seems like 100 years ago, when we were kicking a ball around the playground. Shame about Stewart though, wasn't it."

"All a part of life, Rubber, but old Arthur don't change, look at that photographer's face, I wish I had a camera."

"You do know he does that on purpose, he's quite a clever man, really."

"Who?" I said.

"Arthur."

"You're kidding me."

"No I'm not, we started it when we were at school. First of all, with the teacher, and we just carried it on," said Rubbernose, and added, "we've had years of practice and sometimes I believe he's dense myself, but that man has more A levels than the rest of our class had added all together."

"How many was that?" I asked.

"Counting your one, two," said Rubbernose.

"What did he do when he left school?" I asked.

"He worked for his uncle."

"What as?"

"Don't you know?"

"I wouldn't ask you if I knew, would I."

"He's an undertaker."

"Gord blind me, yes, Walters, that's his surname. I thought it rang a bell.

Can't he get Grim a job?"

Rubbernose went over to get Arthur away, not before going through one of their routines. The photographer didn't know what they were talking about, and called out to Cathy to grab me for the first of the photos.

Then he called for the best man, and Midge came up close to me. We were told to smile. And we both did, and through gritted teeth I said to Midge, "Arthur only turns out to be the undertaker, Midge."

"What have you been drinking?" he said to me, grinning at the photographer and talking without moving his lips.

"Arthur will be able to tell us vou the vone vanger is," I answered, sounding like a bad actor mimicking a German. The photographer was finished with us two, and wanted Cathy and Beth next.

Midge said to me, in broken German, "Vot di vou say about zed Lone Ranger?"

I said, "Arthur's family are undertakers and he works as an accountant for them. We'll be able to find out who the Lone Ranger is."

Midge replied, "I think we'll have to wait until you return from your honeymoon."

"By the time that I get back I shall know who did what and why. That's if anybody did anything to anyone, if you know what I mean."

"If I say yes to that, they'll put me away in the same asylum as you. But I'll chance it and say I know where you're coming from."

The photo session seemed to last forever, especially the crowd one, where everybody has to stand in a half circle. Of course, the last one to gather around, he was busy explaining to our chauffeur a short cut to the Britannia Hotel where the reception was being held, was our dear old Arthur. "Come on Arthur, get a move on," I said to him.

"Daniel Holmes, my dear old china, in all the years that I've known you, I could never understand you."

It all went quiet, everybody listened. This was Arthur speaking, and in a very 'Oxford' style of voice, without stuttering, in the Queen's English, because it had gone quiet and everyone was looking at him. He repeated himself, "I could never understand a word you say, old chap. I wish you and your good lady a long and happy life, God bless you both."

At this moment God stepped forward and said, "I bless you both."

"You two set this up," I said, speaking to God. "I'll get you both back."

The photographer took his group picture. He didn't have to say smile, watch the birdie, or anything else. Arthur and God had everybody beaming.

I had arranged a 36-sweater coach to ferry my guests from the registry office to the Hotel Britannia on the Isle of Dogs, which we were hiring for the reception.

In 15 minutes we were at the Britannia Hotel. We were directed into the Green Room, where we stood around in small crowds sipping sherry and martinis, and friends were coming up to me and Cathy and wishing us luck, and the women were having a close-up of Cathy's dress. Davidson-Smyth had not been able to make it to the registry office, but came up with his wife Luan, who started chatting to Cathy as if she'd know her for years. Quite a likeable person, pleasant, happy, laughable, and very attractive, unlike anything you would have expected, married to Jonathan who for once did not have his briefcase with him, and was missing with Meigui, Xiang Ju and Mudan. God and his wife Bobby, who I think was on her third sherry, and could not wait to dance the night away, and there was Giovanna, wow, Giovanna, didn't she look good. This was the makeover from heaven. Her short topcoat, all white, with the brand name in Chinese all around the hem. The Chinese characters in thin black, and on the pocket the name Meigui, with a little red rose dotting the I's. The real leather handbag, with the same markings, and the shoes to match. The dress was in red, long and sleek, with a slit up one side, pointing up to the mandarin. Neck, again with Chinese characters and a very small bunch of peony flowers and an artistic Mudan! Now my favourite flowers are chrysanthemums, Xiang Ju, and Xiang Ju, I've been told, was a top designer in the underwear industry, and my imagination was working overtime, thinking where one could strategically put their motives, and nonchalantly said to Cathy who, with all the other 'girls', was admiring Giovanna's new illustrious wardrobe, "I suppose the underwear," (by this time I'd already had too much Dutch courage), "the underwear has got luminous chrysanthemums sewn on so that you can see where you're going in the dark."

Xiang Ju saved the day and interrupted, "the kind of nighties I produce we don't need illuminations. We don't wear them in the dark, do we girls? We put the lights on and open the curtains, and these wonderful garments make us even more desirable than we already are. Is that not correct Danny?"

"As long as it doesn't interfere with my football," I said, sidestepping the question.

There were three loud taps on the table by the MC using a small wooden hammer as his gavel. "Ladies and Gentlemen. Please repair to the dining room."

I stood near the dining room entrance with Cathy and received our guests as they entered. One by one they came, hugging, pecking, shaking hands, most of the men telling me what I already knew, that I was a lucky man to be marrying Cathy. Of course there was the exception: Grim. "It's all downhill from now on Danny."

"Thanks. Grim. We promise not to have too good a time, with a bit of luck the beer will run out or we'll have a power cut," I replied.

But Grim had the last word, "A friend of mine died at his wedding. He was dancing the last waltz and he was much younger than you Danny,"

Cathy butted in, "We'll be all right then, and Danny can't dance."

"Yes I can. I dance a lovely conga," and added, "and what about my interpretation of the birdy song."

"I suppose Arthur dances the military one step," said Rubbernose, who was following in line after Grim.

"I'll get you back, all those years you fooled me, the funny thing is, Rubber, I'd met you many times when Arthur wasn't with you, but I'd never spoke to him alone in all the years I've known him. He'll miss doing it; I suppose we won't be able to call him Arthur anymore."

"Good luck Danny. Nice to meet you Mrs Holmes," and looking back at me said, "You're a lucky man, Danny."

They all got to their seats, and the MC asked us to wait, and then hit the table with his gavel and shouted out, "Be upstanding for the bride and groom," and he led Cathy and I to our places at the top table and the champagne began to flow.

After the meal the speeches began, and the best man, Midge, was on his feet. "Gentlemen, thank you for bringing all the lovely ladies along. They all look stunningly lovely. I thought I would start with that, at least half of you, the ladies, will say they enjoyed my speech. But tonight is not all about the lovely ladies, it's about one lovely lady, who I have had the pleasure (long pause), whom I have had the pleasure of knowing since my school days, and who introduced me to Danny Holmes, who I can assure you, that if he'd learnt to snoop and make up stories and lie, would have become a great reporter. But I can assure you, he could do none of these things, but he could write and I have dug up a few of his reports where you will find that he supports the rights of ordinary people. I will spare him the embarrassment of reading them out, but the sort of man you're marrying Cathy, is the kind of man who, on his wedding day this morning, took it upon himself to visit, and offer help, and pay his respects to the family whose business had burnt down and sadly the husband perished in the fire. I apologise, ladies and gentlemen, for not delivering the speech I had prepared but ask you to raise your glasses to two special people."

Midge turned to me and Cathy, winked, said, "Good luck," and sat down. Of course I had to reply so I got to my feet and it all went strangely quiet.

"Friends, Midge, thank you for your kind words. Thank you everybody for coming along. Like Midge, I will not stick to my original reply to the best man's speech and I know that the Wong's would understand, and want us to enjoy and remember this very special day. I lost another friend today with the demise of Arthur. The sad thing about this is, I don't know his real name. Even on his invitation we wrote to Arthur and Rose." This had everyone laughing. "I'd just like to add that as most of you will have heard life as I know it has changed. But had it not changed, - "I was somewhat lost for words but I soldiered on. "What I'm trying to say is that I feel like the happiest man in the world. A lot of you I've known since I was a boy and we are still good friends. Well, we were before you found out I've watered the free beer. But Cathy," I held out my hand to get her to stand, "We would like to thank everybody for coming, an especial thank you to Cathy's brother Tim who gave Cathy away and everyone who helped make our dream come true.

CHAPTER 5

THE HONEYMOON

If you want to clear your head I can recommend it. We were breathing fresh air just strolling along a quiet lane, came within a short distance of the sea shore on the west coast of Ireland in the rugged county of Connemara. No it didn't remind me of Limehouse Reach, not quite the same ambience. No, this is John Wayne country, where 'The Quiet Man' film was made 50 years ago and according to the locals hardly anything has changed.

The previous day we had arrived at the Hotel Carna in Carna Bay. After settling in at the hotel Cathy had arranged to meet a cousin in Cong where 'The Quiet Man' film had been made. We had our photos taken outside the bar where the big fight between the Duke and Victor McClaughlan had started, had lunch in The Quiet Man restaurant, went to see The Quiet Man Bridge, then The Quiet Man cottage, didn't catch a sight of Maureen O'Hara, or Ward Bond and as I said before, if you want to clear your head then go to Connemara. The scenery is breath-taking. I still cannot figure out why they built all these stone walls, I had spent some time wondering if the areas within the walls just marked out what bit of dirt, or was it a maze using stones where no hedge would grow? I suppose if they'd built the stones higher it could become famous like the maze at Hampton Court.

You must excuse me rambling on, it must be the fresh air. "What do you reckon Cathy, why did they build all those stone walls?"

"Maybe it's a kind of defence in case John Wayne returns."

"He's already acted that part in a film," I said.

"What film, I've never seen it, what's it called?" Cathy replied.

"Stonewall Jackson. He took the part of General Jackson. I wonder how he would have solved the riddle of who killed Stewart."

"Even John Wayne could not conquer the Great Wall of China," said Cathy nonchalantly.

"Funnily enough, they've been conquered many times, even after the wall was built."

It was too soon to know whether the Wong's fire was by accident and I have no idea if there was any link to the robbery of the Limehouse Link, Lenny Lomax drug dealings at the Wong's restaurant or if it had any bearing on Stewart's death. But here I was on my honeymoon, relaxing, laying back, and chilling out.

"Let's play a game," Cathy said.

"What game?" I answered.

"It's called Questions and Answers. Now, where can we begin? I know what we know for sure?" said Cathy.

"All right, Stewart died from AIDS, passed on to him by Willy Wong, who was diagnosed 3 months before he was introduced to Stewart," I replied.

"Do we know who introduced him to Stewart?" Cathy asked. "Stewart's boyfriend, who told me all about Willy Wong and was very frightened of anybody finding out that he had told me." I replied.

"Do we know why he was so scared?" she said.

"You're too good at this game, can't we play something else?" I said, and added, "No, I didn't ask him."

"I think he knew a lot more, maybe Stewart confided in him," she said. Reading my mind she added, "Have you still got his phone number?"

"Yes, it's stored in my phone," I replied and started dialling.

The phone rang and the man answered, "Yes, Russell here, how can I help you?"

"Hello Russell, Danny Holmes here, how are you?"

"I got nothing to say to you, so don't call me," and put down the phone. I tried another two times and each time he turned me off. "No chance with our friend Russell, he's been frightened off," I said, and added, "Maybe I should send somebody to see him."

"Let's concentrate on what we know," said Cathy.

"Midge's friends have come up with who paid off Willy Wong's family. It was someone named Chang. Not necessarily linked to Stewart's Chang, but cannot be ruled out," I said.

Cathy was quietly writing down notes in a note book. "The facts we have, Mr Holmes, are as follows. One, Stewart was possibly murdered by Willy Wong. Willy Wong knowingly passing on the virus in a bizarre sexual act. He must have lots of hatred in him to carry it out."

"If I might be allowed to interrupt, Mrs Holmes, would his family have had to be paid by a third party I hasten to add, if he had lots of hatred for Stewart, I think not."

"Let's come back to that," said Cathy, and added, "As there is no indication why a large amount of money is paid by a Mr Chang to the Wong's, could we assume it might have been money paid in lieu of some legal deal between the Chang's and the Wong's. Could it have anything to do with the Links Corporation?"

"Have you ever thought of becoming a lawyer?" I said to her, "and isn't it time you got ready for dinner?"

We got dressed and went downstairs and were well watered and fed and made to feel really relaxed, or was that something to do with being away from the fast moving life at home in England? After the lovely meal, we decided to visit the local bar, Malloy's, and made our way down from the hotel to the bar. And strolling along like young lovers, well not so young, holding hands, not talking, no we had not had our first row, we were just savouring the magical feeling of walking in the middle of the road without a million vehicles trying to mow you down. When out of the night came this white van, yes they've got them in Ireland too, screeching to a halt with this lout hanging out of the window mouthing off in a foreign language. His body language and finger pointing told me he was not a happy bunny. Where is Beth when you need her, she would have torn him off a strip. He saidhis piece and revving up like a lunatic sped off, just out of earshot of a few choice words from yours truly. "Go on, get on back to where you come from, you foreigners are all the same. Where do you park that van at night, in your mouth!!?"

Cathy looked at me, her face in a somewhat bewildered frown said, "Eh, John Wayne, come down from your high horse, we were in the wrong, we're the foreigners here, now promise me when we go into the bar you'll remember we are in their country and also they only speak Gaelic."

I'd often heard the saying "Old Ireland" and most of it is old, especially this bar. It had the old fireplace, the old lamps showing more shade than light, it had the old bar, old tables, old chairs, even most of the people were old and then some old boy got up and went over to the old Joanna and started to play it, and for the next couple of hours we were thoroughly entertained by people just taking their cue from the pianist when playing their song and everyone prompted them to get up and do their party piece. By the time they got around to singing "Danny Boy" I was on my 4th Guinness, added to the wine at dinner and the fresh air which makes you feel drunk, and felt a hand on my shoulder, I turned around and who should be standing there with hands as large as Pat Jennings was the white van man.

"Sure I'll be having a drink withher, but you're lucky to be alive, it's a good job I was not driving on my own because on my own I drive like a lunatic."

So I quoted him a line from The Quiet Man, "I wouldn't like to drive with you on your own." By the end of the evening, Big Pat (the white van man) and I were up on the mike, murdering "The Wild Colonial Boy". Cathy helped me to stagger back to the hotel and put me to bed and I drifted off to sleep with the sound of a dozen or so choruses of "Innisfree". She told me next day that she had to put a pillow over my head to stop me joining in and that I was sobbing and saying this is the best honeymoon I'd ever had. All I can remember is that song 'Innisfree'.

Next day it was up like a lark, a nice breakfast, and then I had arranged for a car to take us out for the day, to see the sites. We came out of the hotel facing the west coast of Ireland and turned right, northwards towards Innisfree.

The scenery was breath-taking. "How's that song go, '100 shades of green'?" I said.

"It's well out of date, I can get 500 shades of green on my computer," Cathy replied.

"Maybe they should rename it '500 shades of green'," I said, and added, "That bloke Pat frightened the life out of me when he tapped me on the shoulder, I thought it was early doors, and I have not seen any funny little green men, leprechauns, since I been here."

"Maybe John Wayne frightened them off," said Cathy, adding, "It might have been them who built the stone walls."

"Should we stop for a cuppa, Cathy?"

"I was Mrs Holmes yesterday, now it's Cathy."

"I'm sorry Mrs H, slip of the tongue, I'll ask the driver if he knows where there's a nice place to stop."

Being that the driver was less than a million miles away, he just heard and just answered, "I know a nice place not far from here, I'll guarantee you'll like it," and added, "you might even see some little green men, have you got a camera in case?"

"I hope we haven't offended anybody, you know, talking about the little green men."

"No, Sir, I believe the old stories myself, my Granny's sure she seen them, fairies and all. Anyhow it keeps me in work, its harmless fun and what would life be like without dreams?"

By this time we had left what you could call the main highway and was, so the driver told us, on the edge of a National Park. There were forests all around us, we had not seen a car for 30 minutes, the windows were open wide, and the wind was gently brushing my face.

"Would you like to stop just before the bridge, Sir?" the driver asked.

"Yes please."

The car drew up in a small area designated for the site seers. The driver let us out and led us on to this ancient monument bridge crossing a really fast flowing river. It was clear as glass and you could clearly see the bottom and also the fish. "The old folk say that in the old days before the bridge you could cross the river by stepping on one fish to the other, all the way across to the other side without getting their feet wet."

"Yes and the leprechauns used to dance on the fishes' backs," I said

"Do you mind if I use that in me brochure that I'm putting together? The Yanks will love it," the driver said, and added, "Me name's Michael".

"It's not a bit like the River Lea, is it Cathy?"

"No, I've never seen a leprechaun around there, although there was one seen at Limehouse, turned out to be a charity runner, three days after the London Marathon. When challenged, he said he was going to the annual dance at Billingsgate Fish Market. Get it, dancing on fishes' backs."

"Yeah, yeah, I get it, must be the fresh air, but it really is beautiful. We'll call this our bridge and each year we'll come back and count the fish."

"In less than 10 years there will be a McDonalds were the car park is and this will look just like the River Lea," said Cathy, but added, "It would be nice to return each year."

"Now time for some sustenance, where's the hotel Michael? I could eat a horse."

After lunch we decided to get to Innis free sooner rather than later, that way we could book into a hotel and stay the night, rather than drive back the same day.

"We are thinking of booking into a hotel Michael. Can you stay overnight or have you got to get back?"

"I'm like a credit card, flexible Sir, but I must phone the boss and my governor."

"Do you know a good restaurant, Michael?" said Cathy.

"For 28 years, that's before you were born." he said with a glint in his eye.

"You keep your eyes on the road Michael," I interrupted.

"Of course, he, my father, drove a horse and cart. He could not afford petrol and we did not need the AA. The horse would just keep going, wherever you asked it to go. We're just arriving at the hotel now, Sir."

"Are you staying the night here or coming back in the morning?" I said addressing Michael.

"It all depends what time you need me tomorrow, Sir," said Michael.

"I was thinking of 11 o'clock," I said.

"Then I'll go home and return tomorrow," he replied.

"Is that all right by you, Mrs Holmes?" I said looking for Cathy's approval.

"Sounds good to me," she said and added, "It will give us plenty of time to chill out."

I went to the hotel and booked in for the evening and returned to the car for Cathy. "We're booked in for the night Michael," and holding out a £20 note said, "Take this and I'll see you tomorrow." He took his tip and touched his hat and said, "Goodnight Sir, and thank you. Goodnight, ma'am," and looked at her rather longer than he should have done.

"Goodnight Michael."

Now, why did I notice how long he looked at Cathy? I'm not jealous, well not much.

"He's a very good driver, isn't he darling," she teased. Looks like she knows me better than I know myself.

"He's better still if he kept his eyes on the road," I said, cursing myself for saying out loud what I was thinking to myself. "I never really noticed," she said.

I just found out something, even with a few million in the bank not a lot has changed. Now take the £20 tip. That's how much I would have given him when I was earning £400 a week. I've just booked into a 3 star hotel, honeymooning in Ireland, which I would have done without the money and even got jealous when someone eyed up my girl. My idea of a good night out is with Beth and midge, nothing changed there, and in the pub with a mike in one hand and a pint in the other making an awful job of mimicking Frances Albert, still can't sing. So nothing has changed. Of course there are plenty of pluses. Cathy is back, I'm 100% sure she feels the same about me as I do about her, well I know how I feel and I'm about to find out how she feels.

Whilst my mind was working overtime we had been given the keys to our room and having no baggage whatsoever and just hung up our coats, and Cathy had found the towels and had decided to take a shower, and as I said before I was about to find out how much she loved me and having justjoined the green party and being an upright, better not use that word, being a conservationist and in the interest of saving water, I quickly undressed and volunteered, yes, volunteered to share the shower with Cathy.

"You know Cathy, it would be nice to own a little cottage over here, you know, somewhere we could, at a drop of a hat, just crash out for the weekend, I bet midge and Beth would love it over here, don't you."

"As long as Beth and I could get into Dublin for some retail therapy."

"Are you happy with married life?"

"I'll tell you in ten years, of course I'm happy, but I'll be a lot happier if we could solve and put to rest this Stewart business. I have been thinking about what you said, you know, could it have anything to do with the Links Corporation, and your conclusion is," I'm afraid the answer is yes, on what you've told me, could they, the other four have voted him out?"

"On what grounds?" I said.

"On the grounds that he was gay, maybe they, the Chinese don't go in for all that."

"Well I've always wondered how Eve would have got on if Adam was gay," I said.

"Probably died of frustration," Cathy joked and then got serious, "Or maybe the fact that he was not Chinese."

"I don't think Adam was…"

"Was what - not gay? Of course he wasn't we all would not be here if he was."

"No, not gay, Chinese," I said, poking fun at her.

"All right, clever clogs, if he was not Chinese, how come there's 2 billion Chinese, Indians, Redskins and the rest."

"You forgot the Green people. And the answer is quite easy. They all came from different planets." Christ that was quick thinking, even for me. I gloated to myself.

"What you just said proves what most women know already, men are all aliens."

"I take your point about being voted out, and I believe that they might not have voted him in if they disliked gays or non-Chinese, of course they could see that he was not Chinese, but Lenny Lomax might or could have been sad enough to let them know Stewart was gay after Stewart had been voted in and they never asked me if I was gay or not."

Cathy broke in," Did Davidson what's-his-name approve of you as Stewart's replacement?"

"I'll never know the answer to that question unless I ask him, but I see where you're leading to, did he and the 4 links expect it to go to somebody else?"

Out of the blue, I was thinking about Shang Yang's somewhat flattering speech towards me at the first meeting in Mount Row, where he praised me for defending China's rights in Hong Kong.

Cathy broke the deep thoughts. "Why the silence, Danny, what are you thinking about".

"You know how I told you about my first encounter with the scream; you remember Shang Yang's short speech".

"Yes, so what".

"Well, the reports he was quoting, where I kind of welcomed Hong Kong back to its rightful owners was somewhat misquoted by my editor. But my research into China's history, not by any means my best work. Apart from building a wall and inventing gunpowder or fireworks, one name, which stuck in my mind, is, Shang Yang. Remarkable as it may seem, he was one of the first great legalists who laid the foundation of the Qin administration system. Legalism was based on the idea that man is by nature evil and undisciplined and can only be kept in order by fear and harsh punishments".

"Well", said Cathy, "I know men are undisciplined, but you're not all evil".

"I'm wondering if Shang Yang or Yang Shang, you know they can use their names back to front, is evil enough to use "Willy Wong" to remove Stuart from the equation. Of course Shang Yang, the first legalist, was way back in the 2nd or 3rd century BC, and our Shang Yang may have nothing in common, but I do remember a lot of what he said regarding benevolence and righteousness and taking advantage of opportunities were not my words, but the words written by, I think his name was - I can't remember, I must look it up and check it against the minutes of the meeting".

"What will that prove" said Cathy.

"Your dead right" I replied and added "it would be difficult to prove anything, but I'd really like to know who did what and what for."

There were more questions than answers. The more we found out, the more we came up with blanks. By the end of our honeymoon we were exhausted, no, not what you're thinking, nothing to do with showering. We'd looked at things from every angle, but after we put all of it together there wasn't a lot to suggest except hearsay from Stewart and his ex-boyfriend Russell, who had simply disappeared without trace.

"Can we visit "Blarney Castle" before we go home" Cathy asked.

"Of course we can. Michael will take us", I said, adding, we can go from there to the airport.

So there we were, in the grounds of Blarney castle looking up to where the people lean over backwards to kiss the stone. We joined the Queue and followed up the stone castle steps, I must say, it's quite a climb, somehow Cathy was ahead of me, and a number of people separated us, I signalled to her to keep going and before I'd arrived at the top, Cathy had got talking to another couple, kissed the stone, and was around the other side of the gantry, calling across to me, encouraging me to lay on my back and kiss the stone.

"Give me your hand Mr Holmes" said one of the, I suppose they were safety attendants, so I took his hand, and there I was laying on my back, with my head and shoulders through a hole 70 or 80 feet up in the air with a complete stranger holding my hand, and I looked him in the eye's, Chinese, "How did you know my name?" I asked. "Don't underestimate us Mr Holmes, I can read Chinese, English, Gaelic, and your driving license fell out of your pocket," he said. I kissed the stone and pulled myself back up on to my feet. Thanked him for his help and made my way back to Cathy. I rushed her back to the car, and we headed to the airport.

On the way back from Blarney castle to the airport, Cathy noticed I was very quiet, "What's wrong Danny?" she asked," just a bit of a headache", I lied.

We arrived at the airport, thanked Michael and picked up our tickets from the departure desk. "Are you sure you are alright?" Cathy asked. I told her about the Chinaman, knowing my name, and mentioned the driving license, which, I no longer had, having had it endorsed 8 months ago, for speeding, for the third time, I might add, and although, some bits of paper had fallen out of my pocket, when I laid down to kiss the bloody stone, my name was not on any of it. Without doubt I was being followed.

Someone was tracking my every move, but who and why? It obviously had something to do with 'The Links' organisation, so I returned to Stuart's message to me, in which he said, "I hope it brings you more happiness than it brought me". That surely meant that he was not at all happy that he had been left the property, money and 'The Links' business. I was warned not to even consider being the head of the 'Limehouse Link' in the first threatening letter, and when I was asked to vote myself in or out, it was the deciding vote, so the vote had been taken before three of the four directors had even seen me. I presume they all knew nothing about me, so I wondered what two voted against me. I hope I get the chance to find out.

We had arranged to be picked up at the airport and after landing at Luton, we collected our bags and met God outside the terminal. The honeymoon was coming to its end.

Back in London

And now, six months after the wedding, Cathy and I were just getting on with life. When another letter hit the floor, I'd been fooling myself that it was a hoax, just someone with a grudge, trying to keep the pressure on me. Did I say trying, that's a laugh (when nervous make joke) they had me shaking in my boots. I felt like batsman No 6 coming in at 5 for 45 with Shane Warned on a hat trick, this being their third warning letter. But I've always believed that good comes out of bad..... So, I'll phone Midge.

"Midge, Midge, Danny here, I've had another letter, "Warning" "I can hear, they are getting to you Danny, now pull yourself together, think positive, you are usually very good when under pressure". "I feel like a grape in a press, all the life being squeezed out of me, "Chateau -de-nerves," I replied, trying to put on a brave face. Midge figured out that whoever was warning me must have alsoresented Stuart and his mother being in charge, and assumed that they had done anything to Stuart or indeed his mother, Midge's case was that Stuart and his mum was in control of the business and had the money for quite a number of years, so there's plenty of time for us to solve who did what to whom, and with luck for what reason.

Good old Arthur has told us who the Lone Ranger is or was, a Wendy long, from the old folk's home, near Salmons Lane. A little old lady of 84, they should have a law that countries have, computers with peoples records allowing Joe public to know who's buried where and all about them, of cause Midge and his press boy's would all be out of work.

Midge had checked out Willie Wong whose business had been sold and the money went to his family, when asked, Jonathan knew the girls were named after flowers, or blossom trees, or well, he was not too sure, maybe doves, I must say he'd always been hardworking and very good to me. Meigui and her sisters could not been nicer, always getting Cathy and Beth to wear their garments. Giovanna is well supplied with Xiang underwear, and nighties, they are so good, that Giovanna's husband Eddy is back, this time it seems to stay, which means Giovanna is not so bad tempered and brandy the cat is sulking because I'm sure that he used to enjoy Giovanna shouting and chasing him around the house.

With the death of Mr Wong, the Restaurant is reopening after being gutted by fire, the insurance paid up, Verdict accidental Fire and death. Lenny Lomax died from an overdose, sad really, but he was a sad man, what with his Blackmailing and drug abuse, and I'm back to where I started at Chingford Mount Cemetery visiting Stuart's grave.

"Hello Danny" it was Arthur.

"Good to see you Danny, the wedding was great, you should do it again", he said.

"I was thinking of making it an annual event", I replied.

"Everything ok, you don't need any services, do you?"

"No, No, Arthur, nobodies pegged it," everything is alright.

"Look Danny could you drop in, there is a few things I think will interest you".

"At your convenience Arthur", I said.

"No you'd better come to my home Danny",

"Where's that Arthur". ?

"Do you know Wapping High Street, The Town of Ramsgate pub, just pass there is Pierhead, and I live in No 4 1/2".

"4 1/2, are you kidding"? I laughed

"No, I do everything in halves, that's why you call me Arthur".

"I usually drop in at "The Turks Head Cafe, which is just around the corner from you, they do a wonderful breakfast," but don't tell Cathy that, I am supposed to be watching what I eat, anyhow when shall I call in to see you"?

"I work from home, so anytime that you're passing" said Arthur.

"It's quite important to me, Arthur can you fit me in today"?

"Danny, it's always good to see old friends, I'll look forward to seeing you".

"Thanks Arthur", I'm on my way, see you soon".

I thought I'd leave the office early, get God to drop me of at "The Turks

Head", walk around to 4 1/2 Pierhead, how can you live in an address like that? There I go talking to myself again, "ha Jonathan, if there's anything that you want me to sign in a hurry, I'll do it asap. I want to leave 1 hour early", I said as I popped my head around his office door, "There's nothing that cannot wait until tomorrow Mr Holmes, Sir". I wanted to ask him if he knew Wendy Long, but thought better about not asking him yet," Good Night Jonathan",I said, closing the door behind me.

"Good night Mr Holmes", He answered, without raising his head from a pile of folders, does he never stop?

I phoned God to tell him I was on my way, and sure enough as I opened the door to step out into the street, God was there door open, ready to roll.

"Turks Head Cafe, please God, and I'm meeting a friend, so I will not need you, once you have dropped me off".

Is there a deadline Sir? He asked

"No just normal". I answered. God would always ask if I was in a hurry or not, we had a very good understanding. "Did you ever hear or meet, whilst you were with Stuart, or Mr Graham, a woman named Wendy Long"? There was silence and then God spoke. "Mr Graham asked me not to tell about her".

"Then you have heard of her" I answered

"Yes sir, I have"

"Then tell me what you know" I said, this time seriously,

"Mr Holmes, when my mother needed an operation, Mr Graham gave me the money to pay for it unfortunately she died, when Mr Graham's mother died in that tragic accident, he asked, no begged me not to tell what I heard. I gave him my word, I would not tell a living soul, and I will not, I swore on my mother's grave, and I ain't going back on my word sir".

I let him think over what he had said, long enough to try to confusehimself,and then asked him another question. "Who else knows what you know God"?

"Only the people concerned sir" he answered.

"Alright God, you can relax, I appreciate your loyalty to Stuart, since his death, I have not heard many good things said, concerning him".

By this time we had just passed the Tower of London, turned right into Thomas Moore Street, on into Wapping High Street, over the hump in the road, which used to be a bridge, allowing access into London Docks, of cause the bridge has long gone, the Dock closed off, making way for all the old Wharfs to be turned into Luxury flats and apartments, something for the fat cats to spend their money on, watch what you say, (I'm talking to myself again) I'm a fat cat now, and I suppose Arthur is as well. I was brought back to earth by God saying, "We have arrived Mr Holmes, same time in the morning sir" "yes, thank you God," I said as I closed the car door and stood outside the Turks Head Cafe, until I saw the car turn around the corner out of sight.

I walked down Scandrett Street, towards Wapping High Street, there was a lovely leafy garden on my right, and it looked like the remains of where once stood a church. The other side of the street, the remains of another church its clock steeple still proudly standing, the rest of it demolished and rebuilt into more luxury flats, just past the church, there's a row of 4 houses, the middle two, being a school house, dating back 2 hundred years, interesting little street I thought to myself, as I turned right into Wapping High Street, crossed over, went pass Oliver's Wharf, incidentally they tell me was one of the first, if not the first Wharf to be turned into apartments, how come I'd never seen all this before.

I went past the Town of Ramsgate pub, funny name for a pub in Wapping, but things could be getting funnier, soon I'd be seeing Arthur's 4 1/2?

Going by Arthur's direction, I go past the pub, turn left into Pierhead, walk along towards the river, and on the left you see a passageway in between the houses, go down to the bottom, Arthur. I knocked on the door, and was greeted by Arthur. "Hallow Danny, glad you found it, come on in and I'll get a brew on, or there's something stronger if you prefer".

"Cuppa's fine Arthur, what you doing in this neck of the woods".

"I'm looking after the old place for 6 months whilst the house I've just bought is completely renovated". Said Arthur, and added "it's over two hundred years old, have a look out over the river", and with that he headed out of the room along a passage, and we stepped out,

"Christ you could have waved to the queen as she passed by, if they hadn't written her off, that's Britannia not our queen", I added quickly,

"I feel like royalty living here "Arthur replied.

"My mate midge could be Lancelot" I said

"You'll talking in riddles "Arthur said

"King Arthur" and his knights, you said you feel like royalty",

"Sit down Danny, and I'll tell you what I know.

"I never remembered you as a joker in the park, when we were at school" he said to me, putting a mug of tea down on a small plastic table in front of me.

"Funny that, I couldn't see you growing up to be a undertaker, you were always mucking about, having a laugh",

"That's because I learnt from an early age, you know, with funerals every day, my dad's family being undertakers, most of the family helped out, when I was young I used to clean the Hearst's, I learnt that life is short, you've got to enjoy it."

"Is that why you became an accountant?" I asked,

"No, I stopped being a boy, started to work to pay the bills, and I'm still paying them".

"Right Arthur, what you got to tell me.

"Some time ago, I was at the shop, in commercial Road, you know the funeral parlour, when who should come in, to book a funeral was Graham, it was his stepfather who had died in a fire". We were distracted by the horn or a tug, pulling 8 large barges. By the way they sat up in the water they were empty, returning to the London corporation, just before Southwark Bridge, where all the refuge from the city is dumped into the large barges, where you will see them usually when the tide is going out, fully loaded with refuge, being towed down river to be dumped at sea, funny that, things haven't changed, I remember when I was a boy, up river, or is it down, at Limehouse creek watching, most likely the same tugs, " it don't change a lot, the river, same tugs, although its nowhere as busy as it used to be." I said as I emptied my tea cup.

"What happened next" I asked Arthur.

"Well, we buried Graham's step father, it was not a happy funeral."

"Who's talking in riddles now ", I butted in.

"I meant cordial, dignified, none of the usual sadness, it was all quite hostile, accusations, of cause a lot of what was said, was in Chinese, would you like a top-up?", Arthur asked, "if you're having one, what happened next".

About a year, well less than a year later, Graham's mother died, I saw the paperwork, this time with Graham's name on it, and I met him one morning, he was getting into his car, after having been at the funeral parlour, we stood and spoke for about ten minutes.

"He told me how his mother died, he was so distraught, and accused his Half-sister and another person, a Wendy Long of pushing her down the stairs". "Arthur" I said, "was all this in ear shot of his driver, God?" "he must have heard, most of what was said, his window was open", if I remember correctly" said Arthur.

"Did you know what was on the coroner's report", I asked.

"Accidental Death" he replied.

"Did it make the tabloids" I asked

"A few columns, that's all, I knew that I'd heard her name before, but where is all this leading to Arthur asked.

"Where was she buried", I asked already knowing the answer.

"Up the mount, was that to be near to the Krays." I asked.

"Don't be disrespectful, the Krays have been very good to our business". He laughingly said, and added," we have a standing order with them".

"You didn't finish up standing, if you messed with them" I said.

"My wife's friend Louisa, told me that Wendy Long lived in the old people's flats in Salmon Lane. Louisa was the Manageress, she lived in and knew Wendy very well before she retired and moved away."

"Do you know if she moved very far?" I asked

"She did not move far Danny, do you know Mornington Grove, off of Bow Road?"

"How did you know that Arthur" I asked.

"She's my wife's friend, and have been friends for many years. You know her brothers the Keons."

"Do you think she will talk to me" I asked.

"As soon as you finish your tea, we'll go and see her, she will agree to talk to you only if I am there," he said and added, "How do you feel about that Danny?"

"Suits me fine Arthur, thanks for helping me, I owe you one."

Within fifteen minutes we pulled up outside a block of apartments in Mornington Grove a turning off of Bow Road. You always hear people saying you shouldn't go back, yet I absolutely love driving, walking around the old east end, meeting people, mates, that you have not seen for years.

"Arthur would not let me pay for the "cab" He paid the driver and into this small block of flats we went. The door opened immediately, she was expecting us, and in we went, Arthur introduced us.

"Louisa, this is Danny Holmes, Danny, Louisa."

"Hello Louisa, thanks for seeing me, all I need to ask you is about Wendy Long, you knew her quite well," yes I did know her very well". Louisa said, "what I'm trying to find out is if she told you anything about an accident, if it was an accident, I replied.

"As I said, I know Wendy very well, well enough to know she did not push or hit her!! Arthur stepped forward, "Louisa, Danny did not ask you about that, but I'm sure if you want to impart with what you heard, he'd be happy to hear it".

"Who did what to whom," I asked

"When the police came to the home, I told them Wendy was with me, but it doesn't matter now, because she's dead", Louisa whispered, "I can promise you that the police will not be involved, at least your name will not be mentioned", you have my word", I replied.

"Wendy's friend came to the house," with her stepmother, and after 3 hours returned by herself. She seemed very distracted, and was crying. The little she did tell me that there had been an accident, and the lady, the stepmother had died, in a fall. Some-time after, the police came, they asked me and Wendy the same questions as before, and left, Wendy later told me that the friend and stepmother had had a row, and that the friend pushed the stepmother down the stairs, after hitting her on the back of the head with a piece of iron. The friend made Wendy take the iron bar, hide it under her coat, and leave by the other end of the tunnel. She told Wendy to throw the bar away, and gave her the money for a taxi and go home." "Hang on a moment, did you say tunnel?" I asked.

"Yes she told me they were going to Greenwich" Louisa replied.

"Oh you mean the walkway under the Thames, on the Isle of Dogs"." Greenwich subway"

I closed my eyes, and my mind went back to a beautiful summers day, When we went to Greenwich and looking up those stairs, following Meigui, my eye's transfixed on her ankles, guiding up her body, stopping to admire (That's a better word than lust) and continuing up where our eye's met, "No, No, she could not do it, not my Meigui, not that lovely person, that sweet innocent girl.....

"Danny, Danny, are you alright?" it was Arthur, "Yes, yes, Arthur, I just cannot get my head around it, she could not have done it".

"I asked Wendy over and over again, and she would not change anything, in the end I am sure she was telling the truth".

Louisa answered and added "But there is more, but would you like a drink Alexandra, and you Danny"?, a gin and tonic if you got one, thank you Louisa", and Louisa left the room to get the drinks"

"It's quite a story, is it not ?," Arthur said, "yes it is, Alexandra" I replied, and added "Who was you named after, your dad?", "My dad's name was Charles, but they tell me that the Tallyman's name was Alex, I think I was conceived on the never-never, Arthur answered "those were the days my friend, I don't suppose they do it now", l said. "Yes they do, you can pay off, for your funeral, you insure yourself, "Arthur replied.

Louisa came back with the drinks and handed them to us. "What happened next Louisa"? I asked "Well about two years ago, Wendy's nephew, William came to visit her, apparently he was quite ill, and when he left Wendy was very upset, William had always been in contact with Wendy, visiting from time to time, "Louisa stopped dead. "What's wrong Louisa" Arthur said, "I don't know if to tell you what she said, its all quite shocking and embarrassing", she was struggling to go on, "Take it slowly", I said "I think I'll be able to fill in the bits you want to leave out".

"Wendy said that William had been forced to do a terrible thing". She stopped unable to continue. Arthur stepped forward and put his arms around her". Its alright Louisa "he said" take your time".

"I think you're going to need a strong Brandy Arthur, when you hear what I suspect, she's going to tell us". Louisa butted in "No I'm ok, I want to tell somebody, its been driving me around the bend."

After gathering her composure she continued. "William was forced to do a terrible thing, although his family benefited out of his dreadful deed, After he died, after he carried out his bizarre act, William knew he had an incurable virus, A deadly form of Aids, and he passed it on to somebody here in the neighbourhood".

I butted in "Stuart Graham", "you're kidding Danny, he wasn't batting for the other side, was he"? Arthur blurted out, "how did you know "?

"Its all making some kind of sense now, but Louisa, did Wendy tell you why William was forced into doing such a thing? I asked.

"She said that her friend told William that it was Wendy that knocked her stepmother down the stairs and killed her, and if he did not do what was asked, she would inform the police, William was offered a lot of money, and he gave a large amount to an old boyfriend called Russell, who was the boyfriend of "Stuart", who unfortunately had fallen out with Stuart, because of this, Stuart had stopped giving him money to buy drugs, Russell actually introduced William to Stuart, William did it to defend Wendy".

"Did she, Wendy, ever say why the friend and stepmother were arguing"?

I asked "yes" said Louisa and added, "something to do with the "LIMEHOUSE LINK".

Great, I thought to myself, after all this time its over, must get home and tell the others.

"Louisa, I can't thank you enough and Arthur, I don't deserve friends like you, I'm bursting inside, really happy, I cannot wait to tell Cathy, relief, great".

I downed the remainder of my drink, thanked them both, Arthur said he was waiting for his wife to arrive, and so I said goodbye and left. Walking up to Bow Road, where I could catch a taxi, I was thrilled to bits, at last it was over. I was phoning Midge as I hailed a cab, "Where to mate" The cabbie said," Chigwell mate" I replied," Hello midge, can you get round to my place tonight, with Beth, I've got some great news, no I'll tell you when you get there," "I phoned you this afternoon, where was you" ?, asked midge," I went around to see Arthur's 4 1/2, yes 4 1/2, eh, what, I'll see you later".

The taxi pulled up outside my house, I gave the driver £25 and opening the front door stepped inside, Brandy as usual got round my feet, and I heard Giovanna and Cathy in the kitchen," Good evening ladies, how's your day been.

"Pretty average Mr Holmes", said Giovanna, "The washing machines playing up, the cat knocked the flower pot over and," I stopped her in her tracks

"Alright Giovanna, just another day, yes, this doesn't mean a trip in the Titanic again? I asked

"No Mr Holmes, just kidding, I'll see you tomorrow Mrs H"

"See you Giovanna said" Cathy

"Goodnight Giovanna" I said closing the door behind her.

"Why are you late Danny?"

"I've got Beth and Midge coming around, I got some great news to tell you all", we got a couple of glasses, removed my shoe's and settled down in front of the open fire, and told Cathy all that had gone on. The doorbell rang, it was Beth and Midge, "hello both, Midge give me your coats, Cathy's in the lounge".

"Danny what's this about Arthur's 4 1/2 "Midge said as he entered the lounge, "Have you seen it Cathy" "Don't take no notice Cathy, all men brag" Beth said knowingly, and I opened another bottle of Chateaux Latour, and told them all I knew.

"I suppose," said midge "when this Louisa, said Meigui and her stepmother was arguing about something to do with "The Limehouse Link", Midge was starting to laugh," Louisa thought she meant the Link under Limehouse basin" by this time, with the help of the wine, we were all crying with laughter, Beth kept it going by adding "she didn't know she was talking to the Limehouse Link",

Cathy chimed in "I suppose Meigui is the Limehouse Lynx" and we all rolled about again, but one by one, we looked at each other and the laughter stopped.

My tears of laughter, became tears of sadness, and they all gathered around me, holding me, Cathy was the first to speak, "this doesn't mean you will have to tell the police", Midge like the rest of us was sobering up fast, "I think we should let the dust settle, think about all that has been said, give it a couple of days, or more, get advice before we do anything"

"I was going to say, just the same as Midge," give it time". Let things settle, and sober up", I stammered.

"I got an assignment in the city tomorrow, have you got a taxi number Danny, we'd best be going".

The cab arrived Midge and Beth said their goodnights and the day was coming to an end. Cathy and I went to bed my head hit the pillow and I was wide-awake. You know that rubbish they tell you, about things will look better in the morning, well they don't. By the next morning, the night seemed to last forever, I must have finally dropped off to sleep about 6am this morning, and then brandy the cat was scratching at the door, wanting to go out, to do his business in our neighbour's garden. So up I got ah, hangover, must get some aspirin. After a cup of coffee my head settled, I knew what I had to do, must phone the office, and then go to the cemetery at Chingford Mount. I wanted to find out if they had changed the stone. Somebody had made a mistake, and put Graham Stuart, instead of Stuart Graham. God arrived on time and I told him to take me up the mount. "I will not be too long God", I said, and walked over in between the gravestones. One quick look at the stone told me they'd put things right.

"Well old mate, you can now rest in peace, I don't know whether to let the police know, and I'm sorry it turned out to be Meigui, but its all over, and I'm glad it is". I suppose I'm not the first person to talk to a piece of stone, but I had promised him, I'd find out who was responsible, "oh and by the way, she will pay for what she did to your mum". I looked around and just a few graves away I found Stuarts mums grave it read Judith Chang born 12.11.35 died 6.7.1984. I remembered Stuart's mum, she was a lovely lady, and I am not saying that because she was always giving us money for the pictures, and a bag of chips, unfortunately the last time I spoke to her, was when she warned me off, of seeing Meigui, maybe she would be still alive if they'd let us carry on seeing each other,

"How can I turn Meigui in to the police", I said, speaking to myself.

I arrived at the office, and was surprised to find out that Davidson-Smyth was sick, and would phone in this afternoon, "Morning ladies, anything you want me to do", "could you man the switchboard at lunchtime, its Shirley's birthday, we'd like to take her out for a meal, Jonathan was going to take over ",said the telephonist " yes I'd love to help and you can all have a drink on me, "Thank you Mr Holmes", lunch time came and I was left on my own. This was the first time I had been on my own at the office, it was not that anyone had kept me away, but it seemed that, things were arranged so that I left the office before the others, about 12.45 the phone rang, "Hello can I help you", "City properties here its about 4 1/2 the Pierhead," yes" I said "What about it" "I asked" we wondered if you wanted to sell on, we have somebody really interested". I had to think fast, so I took a chance, "the chap in charge of properties is not here at the moment, can I get him to call you, can you leave your name, "just tell Jonathan, Michael called, he knows me well", "Right will do " and Michael rang off.

"Midge, sorry to trouble you, can you talk" "yes Danny what's wrong"?

"Could you dig out all the print, when Stuart's mum was killed", "Yes Danny why" asked Midge. "By chance I was manning the phone at lunchtime, and an estate agent phoned me, you're not going to believe this, he told me they had a buyer for, wait for it, 4 1/2 Pierhead". The phone went quiet.

"Midge, Midge, are you still there?" I shouted. "I'm just thinking Danny, this means Arthur's involved". Midge replied "It means they are all bloody involved, Jonathan, bloody everybody, even God" I said. "How much time do you think we've got Danny" said Midge, "You don't have to stay the course Midge" I said "we're in this to the death, if I can have the full story for my editor", said Midge.

"Maybe I can meet you with your editor, as soon as I can get away" I said. "If you are sure Danny, that is what you want", give me a call, and I'll tell you where".

Thanks Midge, thanks a million".

The next day ....

"Hi Midge, sorry I'm a little late, I had to get rid of God, without him guessing anything's wrong". "Danny I got all that was printed concerning Mrs Chang's accident", but there's no mention of Meigui or Wendy".

"There's more I've got to tell you Midge, I'm quite sure, and relieved Meigui was not at the Greenwich Subway that day, that's if the date of her, Graham's mum death is different, to the date on the newspapers, which is?

"The 6th July 1984", said Midge, and added 9 O'clock in the morning" "Well at least the dates match". "How do you know Meigui was not there? Midge asked.

"Because that was the day Cathy and me, saw Graham in Hong Kong, and he said that Meigui and him, had a big row, he never even knew his mother was dead, he had just left her, when I arrived at the Hotel, where we had arranged to meet",

"What about the time difference between here and Hong Kong, said Midge".

"Crumbs, I did not think about that, let's look at what you've got, any photo's", I said,"

Just the same face, on 2 different columns", Midge said, and added, "Have a look, it looks like her".

I took the photos from him, looked at one, and then the other, "Yes Midge it is Meigui, but these do not mean it was her who did it",

"Danny I'm with you all the way with this, but you must not let your heart rule your head". Midge replied.

"Midge have another look at these photographs, what do you see?" I asked him.

"Meigui nothing else", Midge said "and added, what else is there?"

"Forsythia, and a lot of bare branches"", I said.

"So what" Midge said,

"Forsythia in July and the other plants not even budding. That's what," I said. Getting angry, and quickly added, "that might be a photograph of Meigui, but it was not taken that day, it was taken in March or April. Stuart's mum died in July."

"That does not necessarily clear her, but you have got some more evidence concerning one of your friends, and god, and Davidson what's-his name", said Midge.

"God told me his mother died, and yet his wife said they had left the kids with "Gods mother, to allow them to come to the Wedding". I was reading my notes, "Rather', I don't know why, probably something to do with debt, Arthur mentioned still paying bills, and was living in a house owned, by whom, I'm not sure, might even have been brought with the companies money, he told me he's friend let him live there, for 6 months until his house was renovated, 4 1/2 Pierhead was purchased by Davidson-Smyth, who might even as we speak already know that I know he knows, "oh you know what I mean".

After a long pause I continued, "and then Louisa, Arthur's friend, and Wendy's housekeeper, said she was at Wendy's funeral, and last night trying to sleep I pictured that funeral, in fact I'll never forget it, it was so sad, one hearse, the Priest, and one little old lady. Louisa was bloody 6 feet tall, she must have grown 12 inches ".

"Back to God, the so, oh so loyal God. Arthur said when he spoke to Stuart regarding his mum's funeral, God heard every word, and also

Arthur sounded shocked when I told him Stuart was gay, unless the death certificates had been got at".

"Danny meet my editor, Jim, Danny Holmes, "The Limehouse Link".

"Hello Danny, Midge told me a very little piece of your story, I take it you would not be here if you had any other choice. "That's right Jim, I think I'm in too deep, and need help". I told him "I've been keeping my eyes and ears open, and Midge has been seeking a lot of answer's, faxing, photocopying, colleagues have been asking questions "said Jim. "Who's been spreading gossip? " Midge said.

"Nether you mind, your amongst friends Midge, you too Danny, we can help you with our legal team, and get dates, death certificates or any other item, such as passports who's been where, and with whom." and added "But we want an exclusive".

"What do you think Midge" I asked, "I think, no I know, it would be best to have these people behind you, just in case it turned ugly, said midge. "Can we stop the guy from phoning Davidson-Smyth, the Estate Agent from City Properties, Michael", I replied.

"What's his interest", Jim asked.

"It was him, who phoned me regarding a property, 4 1/2 Pierhead, if he lets Davidson-Smyth know I'm on to him, I don't know what will happen" I said.

"Just give the word, and I'll warn him off, if he's not already told him" Jim said."

"How can you do that" I asked,

"We can make a deal to give some free excellent publicity, or maybe go the other way" Jim said. "Let's do it", said Jim and added, "You will have to let me know everything you know Danny, my people will instinctively know what they want, Midge it will be your story, but keep me in contact at all times. Danny the police will have to be informed, but not until we're in position, whatever happens Danny, carry on as if nothing has happened, that is if we can get Michael in City Properties on our side, we will have to move fast".

I arrived home about 8.30 in the evening; Cathy fortunately was stopping the night at Beth's. I'd just made myself a cuppa, sat down and the phone rang. "Danny Holmes, hello Jonathan, you feeling any better?"

"I'm afraid not sir, I've to go for some treatment, I shall be away for a few days, hospitalized, I've been to the office to collect some folders, you know me, I cannot let things mount up, you have my number, and I'm sorry, if there's anything you need, don't hesitate to ring me Mr Holmes, and",

I butted in "Jonathan, you must for once put yourself first, now you do what you got to do, and that is to get well, if there's anything you or family need, just phone me".

"Thank you very much sir, I will. Let you know my results, you will be the second person after my wife".

"Good luck Jonathan". I'm no good at this, I actually felt sorry for him, I wonder what files he took, the ones with the purchase of 4 1/2 Pierhead, I'll bet, which brings me to my old friend Arthur. How do I find out about Arthur, without him alerting Davidson-Smyth, if he doesn't already know. Just then the phone rang, "hello, oh its you Midge, I was just going to call you,"

"Hi Danny, just to let you know, we've put a tail on, Davidson-Smyth Arthur and Louisa." There's been some action at your office, you nearly did not have an office, the fire brigade got there on time, Jonathan is a likely suspect, it happened 30 minutes after he left, with a pile of files, and our friend God helped him".

"That's why I was going to call you, Jonathan phoned to say he'd been to the office and collected some files, apparently he's been admitted to some hospital or clinic, I think for some tests, and would be away for 2 or 3 days, I didn't even ask him what was wrong with him". "He's now at the private hospital in Paddington",

"Don't forget Danny, until we know otherwise, assume the worst, I got a guard on you, just in case".

"That must be the chap in the BT van who's been sitting outside my gate for a couple of hours" I said.

"Don't open the door to anyone Danny, my guy was told to cover you 30 minutes ago, he could not have reached you yet," Midge said.

"All right Midge, I'll keep on my guard" I replied. The night passed without any trouble, but I overslept, I was awakened by the main door closing, and I jumped out of bed and rushed down the stairs, in my underwear, just in time to bump into Giovanna, coming out of the kitchen,

"Its too cold to go out like that, Mr Holmes, and you'll need an umbrella "she shouted"

"Sorry Giovanna, I thought you were somebody breaking in "I stammered, rushing back up to put some cloths on, and realizing I was late.

The doorbell rang, and I heard God speaking to Giovanna, I got dressed as quickly as I could and went downstairs.

"Good morning, Mr Holmes", God said,

"Good morning God" I replied, Cathy will be back midday Giovanna,

"Ok Mr Holmes, she replied

"Come on God", lets hit the road, I'm afraid the office nearly burnt down last night,"

"I was there with Mr Davidson-Smyth last night sir, we took some files, I was with him when he phoned you" God Said.

"How did he seem to you God", I asked, you know Mr Davidson, he just gets on with life, I think he'd feel worst if he had no paperwork to do sir".

"I reckon you know him fairly well God," I said, looking for a response,

"Yes sir, I reckon I do"...

We arrived at Mount Row, the office, and was met on the door by a security Guard, "Can I help you sir"?the guard asked

"I'm Mr Holmes,"

"Right Mr Holmes, you're on the list, you're all in sir, do you want me to wait for the locksmith, and then sign off, sir,"

"Who called you out", I said to the guard,

"We were alerted by the alarm going off sir". We contacted the key holder, who gives us our orders"; "I just have to get my timesheet signed." He replied,"

"If you would wait about until the locks and door is repaired, I'll sign the paperwork", I said, and went into the hallway up the stairs, and was met at the top of the stairs by sally the secretary,

"Good morning Mr Holmes"

"What's the damage" I asked"

"It looks a lot worse than it is sir, but could have been a lot worse, the firemen had to break into Mr Davidson-Smiths office, where the fire seemed to be, fortunately the fire brigade was here, 2 minutes after the anonymous phone call, apparently they were out on a false alarm just around the corner in the next street, otherwise", she said.

"Lets have a look at the damage"? I said, and headed for Jonathan's office, oh what a mess" I said, and added "Have the fire brigade contacted us, is it OK to touch anything, I think I'll phone them", which I did, a discovered that the fire was started by intruders, who set the alarms off, by forcing their way in through the window, started the fire, then pressed the fire alarm button, on their way out. "Have the police been called" I asked,

"Yes Mr Davidson, called first thing this morning, he asked me, to get you to call him, I have a special Number, here sir, apparently he's not allowed, to make call's".

I took the number from her, and walked into my office, and made the call.

"Jonathan, its Danny, how are you?", I asked

"I have not had the Biopsies yet, and they are making other tests. You have seen the extent of the fire, the police and the fire officer, have been and carried out their investigations, they both say it is obvious the intruders knew what they were after, I only hope whatever it was they wanted, was what I took away last night, although it was a waste of time, the doctors will not let me work on anything, while I remain here".

"And right they are Jonathan, you have got to rest and get well", and added, "I'll keep in touch, good luck", I must phone Midge, "Midge Danny here, I'm at the office, its in a bit of a mess, intruders, no I don't know what they were looking for, Jonathan's in hospital having tests, I've just talked to him, no, he's still having tests. "How are things with you", (I was talking like this in case somebody was listening),

Midge answered. We know he went into the hospital, but we think he left by the back door, your man Arthur is away from his wife, bad debts. Gambling, Louisa is his current girlfriend's mother, and you'll be happy to know Meigui was in Hong Kong, at the date you mentioned, which of cause is Cathy's birthday, that's what you were doing there, and you have set a precedence, and Beth expects to go there when her birthday arrives". "That's not quite true, it was part work and part pleasure", I replied, and added quickly as I heard somebody approaching the door". I'll think about what you have said, and ring you back".

We all helped to clear up Jonathan's office, removing files and the small electrical equipment. An engineer came in and moved Jonathan's computer equipment into another room. God was eager to help, and by the end of the day the room was empty, ready for the insurance chap to give us the ok, to get repairs done.

"It's been a hard day God, Thanks very much for your help, I'll see that you're rewarded". "A bit of hard work is good for me sir, same time in the morning". "Yes thank you, same time", and off he went. It had been a quiet ride home, God had been strangely quiet, for him, and my mind was working overtime. Yes you know the score by now, sort out the facts from fiction. So here goes. I get indoors, Giovanna had left for the day, brandy came running over, it was either he liked to see me, or he was trying to trip me up, running in between and around my legs," "I'm home" I shouted,

"I'll be right down, do you want to eat right away or wait, Cathy said, "if its nearly ready I'll have it now" I answered", if not I'll have a shower and eat later, and if you want to shower with me, I'll tell you all about my day", I shouted up.

"I've had a shower, thank you, dinner will not be long, so let's hear what's been going on". In no time at all we were sitting down to dinner, and I was going over the last couple of days.

The phone rang, it was Midge, "Hi Danny just to let you know Xiang, was with Meigui in Hong Kong, so it leaves Mudan. The eldest sister, in the press reports it said Meigui, but police questioned Mudan, it did not matter at the time because accidental death was reported on the death certificate". "Now-a-days the Greenwich tunnel has got cctv, but there was nothing like that then," "Thanks for that Midge I'll have to find another place to murder somebody", "what else have you got Midge"?,

"Its not what we have, but have not got, there is no trace what-so-ever of our Wendy, Midge said. "What's that Arthur got himself into"? I said, and added "He had better have a good story, who the hell did they bury then". Midge broke in, "I think we should have a meeting with my editor Jim, and then take what we have to the police". "There's just one thing Midge, did you get a list of names of other residents at Wendy's last address".

"What are we looking for Danny?" said Midge,

"See if any of them recognize Wendy. In case she was booked in by another name".

"Good thinking" Danny, "Midge said, adding "I'll get on to it, see you soon".

I never did believe her story, anyhow Midge, see what you come up with and we will meet with Jim. "I replied, and put down the phone.

The following day was Midge's birthday, and I wanted a good excuse to leave the office early to meet his editor Jim Appicella. I got God to drop me of at the Eastern hotel, which of cause is no longer open, its been closed down for years. "Drop me outside Barclays Bank or the corner of Burdett Road, opposite the Eastern hotel", "there's no bank near the eastern sir", God replied, "drop me hear on your left God. The Bank on the corner was a thriving bank once, and they used to have the cafe on wheels, on the Island in the middle of the road, until some yobbo's, they did not call them yobbo's then, they took the chocks away from his wheel and pushed it down the side street".

"Did he find it there the next morning Mr Holmes"? "No god, he was still in it when they pushed it".

"I'll see you on Monday God, Jonathan should be back by then". "I hope he is ok sir, Good night sir," I let God get way out of site, and hailed a cab," Canary Wharf please driver", "Righto guv".

The cab did an Ali-shuffle in front of a bus and lorry, went past the Eastern on his left, down towards Charlie Browns, and the West India Docks gates, and, sorry I'm lost.

This was the centre of my three mile world, when I was a kid, this is where Graham, Meigui and me, knew every street, back alley, in the neighbourhood, yet I was at a loss to where I was, in less than 5 minutes we were outside Canary Wharf, I paid the Cabbie, and heard Midge, calling me. "Hi Midge, had a nice day" I asked. "I think so Danny" He said and led the way to his office's. "Happyfellas might be a bit late" "who" I said. Appicella, Jim Appicella" Said Midge, adding "This way Danny, want a coffee?" and with that, he poured two cups handing one to me. "Thanks Midge, how did the photo go down? " You were right Danny, Wong and Chang same person, said Midge, the door opened and in came "Happyfella" and a rather good looking young lady, Midge introduced me, you know Jim, Jacky Allen our Legal person, Danny Holmes, the Limehouse Link.

Right said Jim, "Danny if you could fill us in" "where do you want me to start"? I asked at the beginning he replied.

"I am a local lad, born and bred in "Limehouse" I hung around with Stuart Graham and his half-sister Meigui when we were very young. Stuart's mother Judith married Meigui's father Mr Chang, a very wealthy Chinaman; his first wife had died, leaving Meigui, Xiagi and Mudan. The sisters had no photograph of their mother, even though they were not allowed to mention their mother, even though they were too young to remember her. Meigui told me this when we were very young. As we grew up Meigui and I fell in Love, but were not allowed, to continue seeing each other, they, the Chinese even had me beaten up to keep me away. I joined the army, after Meigui was sent to China. I met Cathy my wife, and went to Hong Kong for a birthday treat to her, on 6.7.84, that date is not only my wife's birthday, it was the day Stuart's mother was killed, the death certificate shows accidental death no actual evidence can be found. The newspaper cutting shows a picture of Meigui, at the time of the accident. But Meigui was in Hong Kong, the photos of her were taken in February/March. There was one leafy bush and all the other bushes and flowers in the photos were just starting to Bud, it was forsythia, that lovely yellow leafy plant, the first leaves of the year."

When we bumped into Stuart he was dressed differently than when I knew him, and had make-up on, I realized for the first time that he was gay. I arranged to meet, I asked him why he did not return my phone calls, concerning the death of his stepfather Mr Chang. You see I had had a phone call from graham a few years back, asking me to be an alibi for him, he asked if I would tell the police if they asked, that he was with me on the night his stepfather died in a fire in a Chinese restaurant they owned. I did what he asked, one phone call from the police, and when I checked up to see what it was all about and learnt his stepfather had died. I wanted to ask him what happened. As I said I had not seen him since, and he told me they had had a fight, and that the pot on the stove filled with fat caught fire and the stepfather was going to tell, Stuart's mum and his half-sisters, did not know that he was gay, I asked if he'd seen Meigui he told me they'd argued the same day. He asked me if I was going to turn him in, I said no, after he promised me it was an accident, the next time I saw him was at Chingford Mount. And yes that is where they buried Ronnie Kray. We were in the prince regent Woodford, and a brief was reading out Stuart Graham's last will and testament, I nipped out to spend a penny, when I came back into the room I had accumulated 2 1/2 million pounds plus. You see Stuart had left me his entire estate and along with that I was to become "The Limehouse Link" I could tell you a lot more about all that, but to cut things short, I earn another 1/2 Million a year, and more if I want to expand, which I don't.

The brief on that day Mr Jonathan Davidson-Smyth, was and still is the ...... I was cut short by Jacky Allen. "I knew him well, and I know what he represents". Carry on she said, and I continued. "It all started when God that's my chauffeur, told me that Stuart knew he was going to die, because he had a incurable Aids Virus witch he had caught, no, being given by Willie Wong. You see Willie Wong knew he was dying of the virus, and was encouraged, in fact induced with cash, going to his family after he died, to give Stuart the virus. What I want to know is why Willie Wong did his bizarre act with Stuart, and who paid his family. We were led to believe A. He sold his business, B. Life insurance, which would not hold up, as they would not pay out if he, Willie had Aids.

I went on to tell them, how I was given the shares by Stuart to become The Limehouse Link, and how Stuart was blackmailed by Lenny Lomax, after hearing from the broken hearted Russell, Stuart's ex-boyfriend, that he had started the fire that had killed Mr Chang, and then how Lenny had hit me and pinched the Limehouse Link, the resulting blackmail, the Wong's fire, etc. Finally arriving at the last 2 days when I asked my old friend Arthur about Wendy, and I went to see him in 4 1/2 Pierhead, how he deliberately told me lies about Wendy, introducing me to an imposter, who told me a further pack of lies, to get me off the scent, then finding out that Arthur was looking after a million pound, two hundred year old property in Wapping, belonging to, I'm not sure if I own it, or if it was brought with my firms money, or even if Jonathan owns it, and loaned it to my old schoolmate without mentioning it, and Arthur in turn not telling me, the person that owes the house he was looking after was Jonathan's. And also making out that Louisa his girlfriend's mother, was the housekeeper, supposedly at the funeral of Wendy Long.

We might be able to get a confession out of Arthur, get him to own up, before somebody gets at him, said Jim,

"Who else is in the frame Danny"? Asked Jackie Allen,

"I can only think, Jonathan", I replied and added,

"Will I be able to"? I stopped "We won't tell anyone about your alibi for Stuart. Danny, "Jim said.

"Our prime suspect is Jonathan Davidson-Smyth, which I cannot believe" said Jackie Allen, and added "Is there anybody else Danny"? Jackie asked.

"Only Mr Chang the "Hong Kong Link" who was Stuart's stepfather's brother" I said

"And how did he become a link director"? she replied," you can hand it down to family or whoever he thinks is the person for the post, that's about as much as I'm allowed to tell you," I replied, "only to add, "it can benefit voting, if you have control of more than "One Link".

Jim stood up, "What's your gut feeling Midge"

"It changes daily", but we have only just today found out about Mrs Chang, and we have not seen a death certificate, or do we know for sure if she is dead, without digging her up, how's your memory Danny ?" said Midge

"Try Me" I said,

"Jonathan and Mr Chang, do they see eye to eye, what I'm asking his, at meeting's in the same room, will Jonathan treat Mr Chang's, any different to the other, Links you know, the quick glance before answering, anything we can build on".

"Midge you, have hit on something, where the others sit around almost scary-like, the only one I've seen with half of a smile on his face was Mr Chang, there is certainty a bond or some kind between them, and I remember Meigui saying that Jonathan's family firm had been the Chang's lawyers since the early days, maybe as long ago as the Chang's made their money from prostitution, and gambling.

"This could be a great story for us Midge", said Jim, and Jackie added, "The Davidson-Smyth's firm of solicitors has been going for 130 years, maybe even longer, when Jonathans father died, it, The Firm broke up, Jonathan became a one-man band, but before that, they had a bit of a reputation, with the underworld",

"Where do we go from here? " I asked.

"Find out all we can about Mrs Chang's, death cert, Passport, OAP payment book, National Insurance number, Doctor, Mobile phone, invoices, anything at all concerning where she's been and what she's been doing over the last 20, 35 years of her life", said Jim adding, "Find out how much and to whom Arthur owes money to. Also Danny would you be in the position to, and willing to cover his debts. If he came up with the answers?" adding "I have to ask you this now, in case we need the answer in a hurry. "I think as soon as we find out a few things about Arthur, do you think you can get him to meet you Danny"?

"Yes Jim," I said.

"Right then Danny, I'll phone you as soon as we get a lead, and you can book up a meeting with Arthur". Said Midge.

Arthur had arranged to see him the following lunchtime, I met Midge and we went to Alfie's pub, the Railway Tavern, in Grove Road. Arthur was already there, I ordered some beers, and told Midge to join Arthur.

"Hello Arthur, you know Midge by now, "nice to see you Midge", how can I help you Danny"? Said Arthur" I'll just get the drinks in, we can sit over there", I said pointing to a table, I got the drinks and joined them at a table near the corner of the bar, Midge had earlier phoned me, and let me know how much Arthur was in for, and asked if I was willing to go that far. "Here we are, Midge your usual, and a Gin and tonic for me and Arthur". I sat down.

"Now Arthur I'm not here to ask you for any help, I here to offer you some help." "What do you mean said Arthur? "Well, I know the meeting you set up for me with your girlfriends mother Louisa was a Hoax".

I stopped to let Arthur think about what I had said, and he took the bait," then you know the rest?" Arthur said, "about Mr Chang, yes, we know all about him", "and are you going to inform the police", said Arthur "how much are you in for Arthur",? I asked. £60,000, Arthur said "what about assets"? i asked him" I could just about cover it if I sold my house," but I do not want to put my wife out of our house, I was hoping she will take me back". Arthur was in state of shock.

"What could the police have on you Arthur?" asked Midge, "Apart from taking a loan from them to pay of my debts., falsifying some paperwork, I'm afraid of what they may do, said Arthur and added.

"Wendy Long lived off Salmon Lane in a Warden controlled old peoples home. Louisa Keong was the home warden, and my wife's best friend.

"Everything was fine until, Stuart's step-father died, and we buried him up the Mount. Stuart's mum came in and brought a piece of land to bury her husband, Stuart's step-father.

I told the wife I'd seen an old friend, and went on to tell her his mum was left all that money and property. After the Chinaman died, she was telling Louisa and Wendy Long was standing within earshot" before continuing".

Wendy's 3 nieces and a nephew visited, and they were all very sad over the loss of a loved one, we did not know, Wendy or the others had any connection, until I saw them at the funeral parlour, when their father was laying in the chapel of rest at the back of the shop in Commercial Road ".

"What happened after that? " Midge said.

"Wendy was in touch with, her three nieces, their step-mother had been left a lot of money, and she was a changed woman, and was continually arguing with the girls, they had already been sent to mainland China to learn their trades, visiting their father three or four times a year, now that their father was dead their home and fortunes in the hands of the wicked witch, which they now called her, there was not a lot to come back to England for. The nearest relations lived at the 'Green goddess' the Wong family, he went on to tell us that the old women sui Long according to Louise was always cursing the girls stepmother for being nasty and mean to her nieces, so much it had made her ill, and she even threatened to do her harm. "Soon after "Stuart phoned, me and told me that he had cancer, and not much longer to live, he was in a right old state."

"But what did they have on you Arthur"? I asked

"My wife Rose and I were having a rough time, going through a bad spell, I think they call it." He panted, breathed a deep breath and continued. "I had been borrowing money, from the families firm, as the accountant and book–keeper, it was not very hard to bet with money that was floating, and then put it back, without anybody knowing. The bookie phoned me one day, and told me, no more bets, until you pay the £20,000 owing. Add that to the £30,000 spent. I was owing the company £50,000"

"That's one time you wished you had done it by half." I said butting in.

"What happened next?" midge asked.

Arthur told us that the large debt caused trouble between him and his wife; his wife let it all out to Louise, and Wendy, and the next thing he knew was that somebody had brought the debt off the bookmaker, and was putting the squeeze on him. They got Arthur in such a state, he even thought about suicide. Then one day he got a phone call, the person on the phone wanted to meet and discuss payment, and said there was an easy way to get out of the mess. Arthur agreed to meet, but not at home, he did not want his wife to know. The meeting took place at 'Victoria Park' next to the boating lake.

Arthur said he was approached by a Chinaman, who introduced himself as Chang Wang (a good ploy, that, reversing first and surnames, which is often the case in china.) He said he was the head of a large corporation, involving amongst other things debt collecting. Arthur was aware that his debts were rising rapidly, from the initial £20,000, which had risen with interest to £30,000. Mr Wang then suggested that a fair trade could be arranged, where the £50,000 debt could be wiped clean, and Arthur would receive £20,000 in cash, if Arthur could bury a person and alter the paperwork involved.

"I thought he was asking me to bury somebody he had murdered who owed him money, and it was his way of threatening me"

"And was it?" asked midge.

"No it was not a threat, he had not killed anybody, in fact the person to be buried, was still alive, all that time, but was dying" Arthur said Wang went quiet and then told him that the person in question was a personal friend of his, and said he was ashamed to say that he had let her down badly, and that that she'd become so bitter, she was responsible for two tragic deaths.

"And who is this person may I ask?" I asked.

"You know her as Wendy Long, but that is not her real name "Said Arthur.

Arthur said he could not believe Wendy could be responsible for two murders, and that him and his wife had known her for years, and agreed to alter any paperwork involved, and the funeral was rushed forward a couple of days to coincide with Stuart's funeral, it was not until Meigui's name was mentioned. And then Stuart being buried the same day as Wendy, he thought there was some connection. There were still a few matters that

I wanted answers to, "What were you doing in 4 1/2 Pierhead?" I asked Arthur.

"Like I told you, a friend let me stay there"

"Do you know if this friend owns it?"

"He said he did," Arthur answered.

"What is your friend's name, Arthur?" I asked.

"His name is Toby Forrester, and he was in the frowns of selling it. I am staying there, until the sale is completed."

"You said you did the alterations to the paperwork involved, was the money matter settled?" asked midge.

"Yes it was" said Arthur.

I thanked Arthur for telling us, offered to help out financially, and as he had a pressing engagement, he left.

Midge ordered some more drinks, and sat there quietly.

"Have you got enough for a good story?" I asked Midge.

"I'm trying to work out how much mileage we can get out of a corpse, I so much wanted that there would be a Mr Big," Midge replied, "but you can't win them all," he said

"I'm sorry Midge, but I don't buy it, would you pay somebody £60,000, grand for what? Changing a name on a piece of paper, what is he really hiding?"

"How did you say he, if you mean 'Chang Yang' he became the 'Hong Kong link, did he not?" Midge asked.

"I think it was being in the right place at the right time," I said adding,

"Apparently there was a fire, they do like playing with fire, and the shares were to be brought, apparently there were no other takers, so Wang was voted in." I replied.

"Can we find out exactly who, where and when?" Asked Midge.

"Quite easy, I can check the minutes, but before I do, I'll tell Cathy,"

Midge said; oh, and I'll check this 'Toby Forrester' we might come up with something there, and I was thinking Danny, if Arthur's story is not right."

My phone rang and it was Jonathan, and the news from him was not good, apparently he had to have surgery to remove a something or other, and would probably be away for 2 to 3 days," "Jonathan you make sure you are 100% before you come back," I said "There are a few things I need you to sign, Mr Holmes, I've made some notes and my wife will drop them off for you," he said.

"Very good Jonathan, I hope everything is ok, don't forget, don't rush back, make sure that you're really strong enough"

"That was Jonathan, Midge, he's going to be away for two or three days, it will give me time to read the minutes, and look at some dates,"

"But I will have to ask his wife, when she delivers some forms for me to sign, more about his condition, and also if I can pay him a visit, just to see if there really is something wrong with him,"

"That might be the only way Danny, I was told that he went in the main entrance, and that they were positive he left with another person via the car park."

I arrived back at the office at Mount Row "Afternoon Rebecca,"

"Hi Mr Holmes," she replied. Rebecca was the company's secretary, and added "Jonathan's wife left some documents for you to sign, she's sorry she could not wait to see you, she had to rush back to hospital."

"I spoke to Jonathan earlier he said he cannot wait to get back to his desk, has he always been so studious?"

"Ever since he was a young man, I remember the day he started, and I knew his father before him,"

"Go away" I said, "You're not that old" I added quickly "Was Mr Graham and I the only Englishmen to hold an office?"

"I don't really know, let's have a look," and leading me to Jonathan's office she gave the form's Jonathan wanted me to sign, got a bunch of keys out of her pocket and opened a pedestal table drawer, put a large book on the table and opened it for me to look, and said "whilst I'm here I must get some postage stamps,"

"And left the room long enough for me to have a quick look at. 'who's who and when,' Rebecca came back into the room, I'd picked up the papers that Jonathan wanted me to sign,"

"I'd better put this back," she said.

"Were there any others?"

"It all looked Chinese to me," I said, "maybe I should have read it the other way round," and we both smiled. But I'd seen what I had wanted to see; Yang Chang had purchased the shares of a Ti Yang, who had previously brought the shares of a Mr Yang from 1939 to 1944 (2nd world war years.) I could understand shares changing hands in the war years, nobody knowing what the outcome would be, and all the links divided by the war, I saw that I was the 3rd man not Chinese to hold an office, the other two having died in unfortunate circumstances, I think that moment was the exact moment to get out, life was too sweet.

The following Sunday Cathy and midge were both coming to us for the day, and after talking things over with Beth, I decided to tell them that I was walking away.

It was not going to be easy, there were many things to consider, these things had happened on my patch, but before I had taken over, but I could not avoid bringing 'The links' corporation into to disarray without bringing things out into the open, and also 'Arthur' was in trouble, for cooking the books, Midge's editor, Jim Appicella, would not be a Happyfella, if he did not get his story, which I had promised him.

Midge and Beth arrived, and along with Cathy and myself talked over the why's and where-for, and the best ideas we could come up with was-

"Jonathan how are you?" I decided to contact Jonathan and tell him.

Due to an old illness, which had re-appeared, I have decided to sell up my shares and pass them on to him, and see his reaction, I or we had had worked out that, if somebody wanted me out the way, or wanted me to be the 'Lime House Link', I would let them have it. After all I would certainly not pass them on to Cathy, and I had no children, so the easiest way out was to let somebody else have it, I would come out with the money that Stuart had left me, and the house. The Mayfair office and subsided buildings were the property of 'The Links', but all in all I was more than £2,500,000, so I could comfortably live on the interest alone.

It turned out to be the best way out. Jonathan took it all in his stride, thanked me for nominating him for the shares, and said that he would call an extraordinary AGM meeting ASAP, and/or candidate, remind me, he'd needed a signed registration letter, and would advise me as to what I have to sign, I suspected that by the time I'd put the phone down, the forms would be ready for signing. He then said that he would think it's best to meet, he offered to come to the house to go over a number of things, one being a property, 4 1/2 Pierhead that was in process of being brought, for investment, and owing to his illness. He had not mentioned it to me, he felt sure that once I had been over the deal, before exchanging contacts, I'd agree to buy it and use it as offices or sell it on.

"Did you say 4 1/2 Pierhead?" I asked

"Yes, near to Tower Bridge, actually on the river," he answered and added

"Why is there a problem Mr Holmes?"

"No Jonathan, but I've been there, my old friend Arthur, you remember him, the accountant, is staying there, temporarily I might add, until it's sold"

"What a coincidence," Jonathan said adding, "It's a wonderful old building, a one off, and there is another property deal I've entered into, that I would like you to look at before you leave, and ..."

I stopped him short "Will it be necessarily for one to sign now that you are taking over," I interrupted,

"You're forgetting the vote Mr Holmes, they may not, consider me." Jonathan replied "They would have to find a new firm of solicitors, etc. before they voted me in," He replied

"Why could you not wear two hats?" I asked,

"I would have to look into that, before I give you an answer," He replied.

"I'm sure you'll think of someway around it," I said. Before ringing off we arranged to meet at my house to sign any forms, I wished him good health, and placed the phone down on its post. "I think we'll open a bottle of Champagne," I said to the others, but the phone rang, it was Cliff Rabanaeu, or Rubbernose, Arthur's double act partner, and the bearer of bad news. Cathy was the first to talk, "Danny, what's wrong? You've gone white,"

"It's Arthur, he's, he's dead," I stammered. "I think you should let your boss Jim, know about Arthur Midge," I said "and give him an update on what I'm doing," I added.

"I wonder if it was; suicide"?said Midge quietly and added" "When was he found Danny?"

"The day after I was with him, he certainly was not suicide then, even though he told me a pack of lies, but I liked him, always did, it's a terrible shame he got into gambling, now, one way or another it cost him his life."

"I'm quite sure your right to get out Danny," said Cathy.

119

"I think it would be a good idea to get Cathy and yourself over to Ireland, until the dust settles," said Beth

"I'll go as soon as Arthur's laid to rest,"

"Midge this is what I think we should do, but before I do I promised Meigui that I would go to the cemetery to see if Stuart's grave stone had been put into position.

The Next day

"Mr Yang Shang, Danny Holmes here"

"I would very much like to arrange a meeting with you, at Mount Row, if it is at all possible, and would appreciate if we could keep it to ourselves"

The idea was to get Mr Chang, and the Chang's girls, together in the same room, (with hidden microphones.)

The date was set for the following Monday, but first there was Arthur's funeral; which means going all the way back to Chingford Mount, an open verdict, the death certificate showed, but the police were not quite happy with that, and were treating it in any way other than suicide, but they could not get any positive evidence, and were still asking questions, which I soon discovered, when I answered my door, the day before Arthur's funeral.

"We are here to see Danny Holmes," said the rather good looking, 30 to 35 years, who added, "I'm detective, inspector, Sally Stevens," holding up her warrant card." And this is sergeant, Toddy"

Again, this made me try to make a joke out of it," "you don't look a bit like Jack Frost," "and quickly added, "Yes I'm Danny Holmes, what can I, do for you, err, would you like to come in?" And showed them in,

Toddy spoke first. "Do you know a Mr Alexandra Francis, Mr Holmes?"

"Yes I have known him for years, we went to school together, when we were lads, we're burying him tomorrow."

"When was the last time you saw him?" said Toddy

"Last Tuesday afternoon, at Mornington Grove, in Bow,"

"What was the reason for your meeting?" said inspector Sally

"Arthur, that's what we used to call him, because he used to only finish half a sentence,"

"What was the sentence about?"

"No, not one sentence, every sentence, you see, 'rubber' that's Cliff Rabanaeu, would say something, and Arthur would, half answer him, and we would always roll about laughing, because rubber would," and seeing the expression on the detectives faces, added, "You had to have been there."

"I think we'd better get on," said Sally, "what did you say your meeting with Mr Francis was Mr Holmes,"

"He was in some kind of money, difficulties, and I think he wanted to borrow from me," "And did you lend him any" she asked. "I told him I would and he was going to phone me," and added, "Did he leave me a note, or something to let us know why?"

"We cannot disclose any information Mr Holmes, but here is my card, call us if you think of anything you think we should know."

Soon after they left, the phone rang; it was Nibbo Wilson, "Hello Danny, I just got back, and heard about Arthur, he seemed ok when I last saw him, the day before he died, what do you think triggered it off,"

"I find it hard to believe Nibbo, it just doesn't make sense, "But I'll see you there tomorrow, where are you all meeting?""Down Alfie's, most of the lad's will be there, see you about half past one,." "Thanks for phoning Nibbo, I'll see you tomorrow."

CHAPTER 6

ARTHUR'S FUNERAL

Cathy and Beth, had decided not to attend, Midge wanted to come along, apart from showing his respect to Arthur, we might be able to hear any gossip, we got to Alfie's pub, in Grove Road, Bow. ?

A few of the lads were already there, "hi Danny, Midge, what a turn up, what odds would you have got on Arthur doing that," I was Nibbo, he lays odds on everything, His whole life was based on the track and betting.

"It must have been a terrible death," said grim.

"Trust you to think the worst," said Hi-Jack, who had just arrived, "Hello lads, here's to Arthur," he said, holding up his glass, which Alfie had prepared for him, seeing him come through the bar door," hi-hi- jack next time you are having your lorry nicked, make sure Grimm's in it", said Alfie, "My contacts would bring it back, and never deal with me again, if they had five minutes of Grim," said Hi- Jack.

"I wonder where he got the drugs from," said Grim.

"If you find out, let me know my dogs need something to shake them up"

"Tell them if they don't buck there ideas up, you will put Grim in their kennels with them," said Hi-Jack "No, wouldn't work, they say a winning dog is a happy dog, 5 minutes with Grim, the first time you opened the kennels, the dogs would be off, and you will never see them again, "Alfie shouted back.

"What do you think Danny "?Asked Dandruff.

"Who said he was on drugs?" I asked, "That women detective asked me if I knew where he brought his drugs," said Grim

"Arthur would never take drugs," said Nibbo Wilson "hold up there's Rubbernose "He was Arthur's best mate."

"Before you ask, the answer is no-way, Arthur was dead against drugs, there's no-way he took them, and they must have been forced on him, anyhow lad's the funeral's not going ahead, it seems the lady detective, has got a delay." "It seems like Arthur's doing it again, he never finished anything," said Grim.

"Old Arthur would turn in his grave, if he heard you grim, cracking jokes at his expense."

"On what Ground did she stop it all going ahead?," I asked.

"On the grounds that the doctor at the scene of the crime, and knowing Arthur had had some marital and money, troubles, he was treating both Arthur and Rose his wife with stress and nerve problems and the fact a witness has come forward, claiming he was visiting Arthur and saw two Chinese men bundle Arthur into a car, just few a few hours before time of death."

Midge whispered in my ear, that he would pass the information on to his editor Jim Appicella, and sloped out quietly. I ordered another round of drinks. "Make mine a brandy Alfie, and get the lads another," I said softly, yes, I was still slightly embarrassed about having barrels of money, and did not want to appear flash, these guys were my friends when I had nothing, and thinking back I remembered Arthur, did we always call him Arthur, no, I remember we called him 'A', just 'A', I suppose a for Alexander. "Now come on Holmesy, Arthur wouldn't want tears," "it was Grim," It's all right, a lot happened to me over the last twelve months or so, coming back to my roots, meeting the old gang, the rags to riches, getting my girl back, marrying, it all restarted at Stuart's funeral and now it's nose-dived", I always get nostalgic and upset when I have a beer, or two, at the point Midge came back. "We have got a meeting with Jim tonight, if you're up to it." After saying our farewells, Midge and I went outside and Midge, has always called a cab out of the blue, and off we went," "Reuters, Canary Wharf please mate."

'Happyfella' (Jim Appicella.) was looking his usual self, which was strained and agitated, whereas most men like a drink or a women or two, and get withdrawal syndromes if they go without, with 'Happyfella' it was a headline, a front page story, that was like a drug to him, and an exclusive treble murder, this was something out of this world, "Midge, midge we must not spoil this, we must handle this properly," Jim said, and added, "I'm sorry to hear that you cannot carry on with 'the links,' Danny" " I like breathing too much, no disrespects, I don't fancy making the front pages" I replied adding, "I'd like 24 hours to try to find out who was responsible for three deaths," I continued telling him that I had a plan, and after a bit of an argument, it was agreed that the meeting I had arranged with Yang Chang, and the three Chang sisters and Jonathan, would go ahead. The fact that I had visited a local shop in Mayfair. Just around the corner of Mount Street, this shop was full up with all the latest bugging devices, and in Jonathan's absence, with the meeting arranged, I'd asked the shop's engineer's to bug the most likely rooms, I was scared and did not want to take too many chances, in case things went wrong.

'Jacky?' the solicitor, who knew Jonathan Davidson-Smyth stood up and said, "Danny just a word of caution, don't trust any of them, and do you recall telling us Meigui was in Hong Kong at the time of Mr Chang's death?"

"That's correct, her and Stuart had a row," I answered quickly "Could that argument have taken place over the phone?" she said, or asked, her manner confusing me, and I was getting annoyed, protecting Meigui, " I assumed that it was face to face, but it could have been by phone, and she was in Hong Kong according to midge". " Midge 'piped in'" my contacts told me her passbook was in Hong Kong, but the latest report suggests that Meigui was in fact in London with a certain Jonathan Davidson-Smyth, I'm sorry Danny, but I am having it rubber stamped, to make sure there's no mistake, I'm still hoping there's some mix up,"

Happyfella asked, " How can we listen in to the conversation Danny," " There's a car park at the rear of the building, the engineers have a van parked there to receive cameras and microphones," I answered " I like your style," said Happyfella, he's face actually smiling, adding, "Who do you think the No 1 suspect is?"

"I think its Yang Chang, but your latest bombshell, concerning Meigui and Jonathan, gives me some doubts," I answered, feeling quite rattled.

Mr Chang was sitting patiently in his car with his two companions, both of Chinese origins, who looked like a couple of heavies, or bodyguards. Arriving by cab, I paid the fare and approached the main door to the office in Mount Row Mayfair. I quickly opened the door and entered the small room to turn off the alarm, went back to the front door in time to greet Mr Chang.

"Mr Chang, so glad that you could find time, I have asked Mr Davidson-Smyth to attend," And Jonathan arrived exactly at the right time. "Please show Mr Chang up Jonathan, (Allowing him to go to any part of the building he chose.) I'm just using the bathroom, they made their way upstairs in time for me to reach the main door, just in time to meet the three sisters, Meigui, Mudan and Xiang.

"Hi girls, I'm delighted you came, could you all be very quiet, I have a surprise for you all, follow me, now quietly please and I led them to the room of Jonathan's choosing,"

I walked in, and guided the girls to the conference table, "Gentlemen, let me introduce the Chang sisters, you are their uncle Mr Chang, will you tell them who their mother is, or do I?".

Jonathan stood up and blurted out, "Mr Holmes, you have no right, it is their business and their culture, I", Jonathans stopped at this point Wang Chang rose to his feet.

"Jonathan, it's quite all right, I have given my solemn promise that I would not reveal to anybody, I gave her my word, and have lived to regret it for many, many years, but believe me girls, I could not tell you, with tears in his eyes, Yang Chang whispered " I gave her my word."

You can imagine the girls, they stood there looking at me, and Meigui was the first to speak. "Danny, please, please tell us please," Just as I was about to speak Mudan said, "Our mother was, 'Sue Wong' and looking at Yang Shang said, "And you are my real father." Her two sisters, looked at her in disbelief, Meigui said, "Is he also our father?"

"No," said Mudan, adding "I was conceived before it was agreed, by our grandparents, that Sue Wong should marry Yang Shang's brother so you see Sue Wong and Yang Shang were," Yang Shang rose to his feet, holding up his arms as if he was telling everyone to stop and listen." It is written, that obedience to your parents and elders is paramount, it is customary that they lead, and we follow. He took a deep breath before continuing.

"You see, I was advised, no instructed, not to have any contact with Sue Wong. They told me she had been promised by my eldest brother, they said that my feelings of total love, that I still have, would die, like the blossom, without water."

There was a complete silence in the room Yang continued, "We were young, we were in love, both our parents called it headstrong," he stopped, and looking at me said, "Mr Holmes why have you brought us all here, it is not to hear our family history?," "My sincere apologies Mr Chang, I could think of no other way of getting or finding the truth, and I might add, I am very frightened, in fact scared out of my life,"

Mr Shang answered, "Who are you scared of Mr Holmes?"

"I hope to find out today."

"Why do you need me here?" Jonathan asked.

"Simply I have never had a meeting without you, I might need your help, and there's just one thing I would like to ask you, how did you know about the warning letters that I'd received?," there was a quick eye-to-eye glance from Jonathan to Yang Chang.

"I knew Mr Graham had some bad mail from an unknown head case, but I do not recall any conversation concerning warning letters" He said and added, "is this what all this is about?."

"No" I said, and added

"That is not all, I would like to know why Stuart was killed, and also what really happened to his mother?" the silence was deafening.

Mr Chang was the first to speak "Mr Holmes, I was in China when I heard the grave news of my brother's wife accident," Mudan butted in "I was with them, but a little way in front of my step mother and, she stopped "Who was with you?" I asked, Mudan continued "Sue Wong was directly behind her, I heard my stepmother cry out 'Don't' and then went crashing and stumbling past me, banging her head on the wall, and then a horrible crack as her head hit the bottom step." Mudan went quiet and tears ran down from her eyes, "What happened then?" I asked. "Sue Wong came up to me and said, that for special reasons I should not tell anyone she was there, she told me to wait a few minutes, then go back upstairs to get some help, whilst she would leave at the 'Greenwich' end of the tunnel. Everything happened so fast, I did as I was told and after a few minutes, I returned to the top to raise the alarm." "The ambulance came and they told me she was dead and the police came, and asked me questions, once I told them we were alone, I have to stick to it." She was really sobbing now, and her sisters put their arms around her to comfort her.

After a little while, I asked Mudan how she knew Sue Wong was their mother. She said that when Stuart became ill, and called her and her sisters, to tell him he was dying, she was in the Limehouse area, and went to see Sue Wong.

Sue Wong was very ill and made me promise not to tell a living soul, Mudan could hardly get the words out, and took a photo out of her handbag "Sue Wong, my mother gave me this photograph, it was of her and me when I was just a few weeks old, and I have one each for my sisters, when they were just born, she told me that she was our mother. But Yang Shang was my father, and Wah Shang, her husband, found out and threw her out, strange as it might seem, he forgave Yang his brother,"

The girls were looking at Yang Shang, waiting for him to deny it, but Yang stood up and said, "My journey through life has been, at times, very traumatic, but nothing can compare with the love I had with Sue Wong, and the heartache we shared, knowing Mudan was our child, and not being able to share our lives together, all three of us, even now, I cannot put my arms around you Mudan, without feeling guilty, and bringing shame to my dead brother, Wah, who I loved dearly." His head was hung forward and he was having difficulty finding his words. He regained his composure, and looking at me said, "Mr Holmes, Sue Wong was responsible for the death of my sister in- law, but I trulybelieved her when she told me it was an accident. Sue Wong's version of events were, that she and Judith, were arguing, and tempers were raised, she said Judith lashed out at her, and she defended herself the only way she knew, ju-jitsu, catching Judith off guard and off balance, a simple ti-toshi, definitely not to be used, whilst ascending stairs, but frequently used in self-defence, in this instance it proved to be fatal," "And you were prepared to pay £60,000, to protect your name?" I said.

Yang Chang looked blank, "What are you talking about Mr Holmes?"

"The sixty grand you paid my old friend Arthur, to keep it all quiet, and change the register," I answered.

"I have no knowledge of any friend, and have not paid anybody £60,000 to keep quiet, "But you have my word, I will assist you in finding the truth," Jonathan stood up and said, "I don't think I can be of any help gentlemen, I have urgent engagement, please excuse me." And went to leave,

"There are a few questions I'd like to ask you before you go Jonathan" I said.

"If you could make it quick," He answered

"Were you being blackmailed Jonathan?" I asked

"No," He stammered and added, "It's none of your business."

"Why was she blackmailing you Jonathan, was it something to do with your relationship with Willy Wong?"

"I don't know what you are talking about," he was shouting now, "My contacts tell me that Sue Wong found out about you from her nephew, Willy Wong, did you blackmail him in to giving Stuart that incurable decease, after you found out that Sue Wong was responsible for Stuart's mother's death, So once he had done his evil deed, he told his aunt, and she threatened to tell Yang Shang, and let you know who she was, that must have come as a terrible shock Jonathan." I said coldly "You cannot prove anything now they are both dead, its all 'hearsay' Jonathan cried out, adding, "And he will end up in jail for fraud" he said pointing to Yang Chang.

Meigui stood up "That's not so, it was me who was blackmailing Jonathan in revenge for our brother Stuart, who gave me 2 letters shortly before he died, one I gave to a man called 'Goufan,' who paid off Arthur. The other I have here," she produced a letter and handed it to me. I read it to myself before looking up, when I did, everybody in the room, was tense and waiting to hear what it said. "To Danny Holmes," I have persuaded Meigui not to show this letter to anybody, unless the occasion arrives that the truth must be known. Willy Wong on his deathbed pleaded with me to forgive him for the inhuman act of passing on his decease to me. Willy was being blackmailed by Jonathan Davidson-Smyth, who had found out Sue Wong was responsible for the death of my mother. My crime was taking Russell off of Jonathan. I have taken no action against Sue Wong, after talking to my three sisters, whom I love dearly, I believed them when they told me, their Aunt, could not have deliberately pushed Mum down the stairs, it must have been an accident. I have asked Goufan to talk to Arthur and persuade him to cover Sue Wong, after learning from Mudan, who Sue Wong was. I think Jonathan would have been proud of my plan, blackmailing him for £60,000 to pay off Arthur's debts. Meigui and Xiang Ju unknown to them were given envelopes from Jonathan's, with money inside to give to Goufan for Arthur, Hence, beware of the flowers.

Jonathan was the first to speak "You cannot prove anything, anybody could have typed that letter, all lies, I'm off, do what you want with it," and went towards the door, "He won't get far, I'm phoning my men now," said Yang Shang. "That's ok I think he'll have a reception party waiting for him," the door buzzer sounded, it was Midge.

"Danny, we have got all that, the police are with Jonathan now, are you coming back with us," "No midge I got something I have just got to do."

The others in the room were chatting away in Chinese, Mudan and Yang Chang looking at each other not daring to reach out and touch.

"Mr Chang, Meigui, Xiang Ju, Mudan please except my sincere apologies, I would not have arranged this meeting if there was any other way.

Ever since I became involved with 'The Limehouse Link' and the warning letters started, hearing about Stuart's death, and his Mum's, and other things, I have been afraid, I thought my life was in danger, I even phoned Jonathan a few days ago and agreed to sign over my half of the shares to him, I was that scared I had decided to get out in one piece, whilst I still had the chance. I now hope this is over, and before we go, another thing I would like you to come with me, all of you, there's something I would like to show you." Yang and the others followed me downstairs to the street; I locked up, hailed a cab, and asked Yang to follow.

We arrived at Chingford Mount Cemetery, and I led the way to Stuart's grave, after buying two bunches of flowers. The others were very quiet, and as we reached Stuart's grave, I placed one bunch of flowers across the stone, and quietly said, "I did what I promised Stuart, and your plan worked." And turning to the others said, "He even planned something for you girls, come this way," I led them across to Sue Wong's grave, and said,

"I still don't know who put the one bunch of flowers on, but I can tell you that you were with Sue Wong your mother, when she was buried, I was here as well at Stuart's funeral 50 yards away."

I wasn't sure if the girls heard me, for they were kneeling on the ground around Sue's grave, actually hugging the stone. Yang Chang stood next to the stone, and put one hand on it and the other around Mudan. The loan manager was back with her family.

I dropped Meigui and Xiang Ju outside the green dragon Chinese restaurant ran by Sue Wong's family, the Wong's, and made my way back to see Midge, and Happyfella, got the lift to the second floor, and then the shock of my life. As I could see the Happyfella office, with 4 people sitting around the room, Midge, Jim Happyfella, Jacky Allan the solicitor, and, well I am a monkey's uncle, Jonathan!

I knocked on the door and went in.

Happyfella turned to me and said, "Danny we have asked Jonathan to come in, and he agreed, the police have questioned him and he has agreed to help us."

"Hello Jonathan, I think we can help each other."

"In what way Mr Holmes?" he replied.

"Arthur told me that Yang Chang brought over the betting debts from a bookmakers and moneylenders, meaning that Arthur now owed Yang Chang, the money. He said Chang offered to wipe the slate clean and gave him money on top; if he would alter the paperwork concerning Sue Wong, and Wendy Long." Adding "Arthur did what Chang asked him and recovered his cash, so I agree with you Jonathan, Stuart did not write the letter, and Meigui did not receive it from Stuart,"

"The letter, can I read it Danny?" Midge asked

"There's only my fingerprints on it Midge," I said holding the letter on the desktop so he and the others could see and read it.

"Somebody has got it in for you Jonathan," said Jacky Allen adding, "Can you think who?"

"I only wish I knew," said Jonathan.

"I think I have solved it, but might have trouble proving anything,"

Taking a deep breath she continued, "I'll have to ask Jonathan first if he was blackmailed? Looking at Jonathan for an answer. He hesitated and answered, "Yes" he said "I told the police somebody was blackmailing me, I was afraid to tell, my wife and family, I have told them now, and I am glad it's out," he said almost ashamedly. "We are taking about your sexuality," Jacky said. "Yes, the other accusations are untrue, lies," Jonathon said.

"According to Stuart's letter Yang Chang could be in trouble, which would leave, one; Meigui or all three sisters as the guilty party, unless Yang Chang was responsible and decided to take a small charge of fraud, and get some sympathy of the court, because of the long association he had with Sue Wong, or it's back to you Jonathan for staging the whole pantomime, but to do that you would have to be in a pact with Meigui and/or her sisters.

Which tells us that, the girls are definitely, or should I say Meigui with or without her sisters is most certainly in trouble. And of cause we must track down Goufan, he holds all of the answers." With that she sat down.

"Midge," said Happyfella "Got any ideas?"

"I could check with god, see if he has heard of Goufan," I butted in, already dialling his, gods, number.

"Hello god, yes it's me, think hard god, did Stuart even mention anybody named 'Goufan', no he never mentioned him to you, but you've heard the name, so, he's a friend of his, is he, thank you,"and putting down the phone, he looked at the others and said, "There is a god," I looked at Jonathan, and they saw I was moving and slightly nodding my head up and down, the others knew that what god had said, had something to do with Jonathan.

"I can explain," Jonathan mumbled.

"I bet you can," I said, and added, "God, my chauffeur, tells me Goufan was a good friend of Jonathan's, and also that he's Meigui's boyfriend.

Jim Happyfella was getting excited, he could smell a triple murder exclusive, Jonathan said, "You are jumping the gun again, because I have a friend named Goufan, Doesn't prove anything." Jim Appicella was on the phone, "George you are at Limehouse, yes it is about that, see you in 5 minutes." Jonathan made a move towards the door, midge moved in front of him, "You're not going anywhere," he said menacing, and Jonathan decided to hang around.

George (Detective Inspector) Morton came in, had a quiet whisper to Happyfella, with a few glances at Jonathan. Before walking up to Jonathan, "I'd like you to accompany me down to Limehouse Station Mr," looking up his notes, "Err Davidson-Smythe. Would you come with me sir?" "I would like to make a phone call to my lawyers." "If you think its necessary sir," answered Inspector Morton, after which they left the building.

Jim Appicella looked at Midge. "We have an exceptional good story here Midge, reaching all around the world, just in time for the weekend. I want at least six full sheets, we already have the background on all parties, the love story, the girls not knowing that they were at their mothers funeral, one of them not knowing her own father. I want pictures of Greenwich walkway under the Thames, the Cutty Sark, mention the Krays at Chingford Mount and the stone with the name on it, what was it, Wendy Long, make the photograph show Wong, I want the whole story don't miss a thing." Get Goufan before he gets to the girls." Midge stepped forward, "We have it all covered already Jim, I'm sorry Danny, but we had to move quickly, and Yang Chang, have alerted your company." Said Midge. "I have already emailed them Midge, telling them to expect some shocks from members of the company and promising them an up-to-date report a.s.a.p., anyway if anyone deserves an exclusive, it's you Midge, thank you for staying with me Midge, and you're a true friend."

Midge looked at me and with a straight face said, "Well you don't know its all your fault, don't you Danny,"

"What do you mean?" I asked

"Well, if you had fancied Stuart instead of Meigui', and if Stuart had not taken Russell away from Jonathan." Midge stopped,

"Are you saying that Jonathan and Meigui got Stuart killed (A) because he stopped Meigui and me, and (B) because he stole Russell from Jonathan.

What about Stuart's mum?" I asked, "Just as Yang Wang told it." Replied Midge. "What about dear old Arthur?" I said and added, "Do we know if it was suicide?" "I'm afraid not Danny, but the police have got a prime suspect, that we hope to reach before they do." "I'm going home to see my wife." I said, adding, "Ring me if you need me." Jacky Allen answered, "I don't want to scare you Mr Holmes, but I think you should have a guard or some kind of protection until we find out who did what and lock them up."

"I think you're right, Midge, could Cathy stay with you and Beth?"

"I have already suggested they do some retail therapy in Dublin," he answered adding, "I said we could be held up here for a few days, I hope you don't mind Danny."

"Of course not Midge, I should have thought about her sooner, they'll be safe there, thanks a million Midge."

"You will be alright Danny, now don't worry, we are going to get Jim the best exclusive he's ever had."

I sat back in the cab, my brain spinning around in my head, I had not been getting anywhere near enough sleep, Christ was I tired, and I dropped off to sleep. "Wake up mate, we're there." Said the cabbie. I put £25 in his hand and said, "Is that enough driver?" "Thanks very much Guv, that will do nicely." And off he went. Brandy the cat did his usual tripping up routine as I opened the door, locked it behind me, and looked at our note board. Sure enough, one from Cathy,

"Dearest Danny,

Checked with bank account, discovered we had money left, so I have gone shopping with Beth in Dublin, see you when the money runs out, be careful.

I love you Cathy.

I felt better knowing Cathy was away from it all. I followed Brandy into the kitchen, checked the doors and windows, and went back towards the front door to put the alarm on. Just as I reached up to set the alarms, the doorbell sounded, foolishly, I opened the door, and it was Meigui. "Danny, I had to see you on your own, I lied to you, and it was Jonathan who gave me the letter, not Stuart." She was sobbing, "We asked him for help with Sue Wong, and he came up with his plan when he discovered Willy Wong and Sue Wong were related. When Mudan told us Sue Wong was our mother, I got confused and decided to give you the letter. When you took us to her grave, I was so upset, I could not tell you, I so much wanted to believe her, she was really crying saying, "Danny, please believe me, you do believe me, don't you?" "Of course I believe you." I said quietly, now let me get you a drink, you stop crying." I went into the green room to get some drinks; I needed one more than she did. "Same as usual?" I shouted back to her, poured her a gin and tonic and then one for myself and reached into my pocket for my mobile.

Returning to the hallway and Meigui, I said, "Now come into the lounge, sit down and we will talk. I put my drink on the coffee table, sat

Meigui down and said, "I'll be right back, I'm just going to change," and made my way upstairs to phone Midge and let them know Meigui was with me. I picked up the phone, in time to hear the line go dead. I broke out into a sweat, usually I can think of something funny to say when I'm afraid, not this time. I crept out of the bedroom, bang, and the next thing I knew was waking up in the hospital. There was Midge, "Come on Danny wake up, and read the headlines." Then I heard Cathy, "Midge, he's coming to, quick call the doctor."

"Mr Holmes you are going to be alright, you are lucky she did not hit you with something heavier." Said the doctor, who was now giving me some tablets to take, "Make sure he takes these tablets Mrs Holmes, we will see how he feels and maybe you can take him home in the morning." My head was hurting, but I tried to get up, which meant it hurt ten times worse. "How was the other guy Midge, did he come off worse?" "The other guy was a lady, not a scratch." "What did she hit me with?" I asked. "You don't want to know." Said Beth.Oh No, not that again!" "I'm afraid so Danny, the "Limehouse Link." "Did you catch him?" I asked. "We caught them, her and Goufan, you had a lucky escape Danny, Goufan, the boyfriend was about to inject you with drugs." Said Midge. "How did anybody know they were there?" I asked. "One of the last things you said was, call me if I needed you, which I did, both your mobile and home lines were cut off, so I called the local Nick, they rushed in just in time to stop the injection. The fact is, he did get some into you, and you have been out of it for two days." Midge replied.

The next day they allowed me to go home, my head was still hurting, my ego bruised, my heart shuddered, my feelings confused, the police had been to collect my full 20 page statement. Meigui and Goufan were charged with attempted murder, of yours truly, her boyfriend, Goufan charged with murder (Arthur.) he was seen with another unknown persons pushing poor old Arthur into a car 2 hours before Arthur was found dead, and with the help of DNA. Goufan was going to prison for a long time.

It turns out that Wendy Long (Sue Wong, Mrs Chang, the girl's mother) told Arthur's wife Rose (the warden) at the home where Wendy lived, about the row and accident resulting in Stuart's mother's death. Wendy confided in Rose and told Rose her life history and who she was to the girls. Wendy claimed that she was still Wah Chang's wife, and that meant Judith was not really married, resulting in Stuart not being the heir to Wah Chang's estate, which he left to me. Now what's all that got to do with Jonathan? Well the part about the row was true, but it was Meigui who had the row and did the pushing. Abbelt by accident or on purpose? Arthur was then approached by Stuart to arrange the burial of his mum Judith. Arthur told Stuart, being an old school friend, about what he had heard, obviously putting two and two together and realised Wendy, Meigui and Stuart were somewhat related. Stuart told Jonathan who made contact with Arthur, and Arthur, having been playing with his family firm's money, and now owing £30,000 in gambling debts, was easy prey for Jonathan, who used Arthur to blackmail Stuart, or he, Arthur would tell about Judith's marriage being bigamy, and with the help of Jonathan, who disliked Stuart immensely because Russell chose Stuart instead of Jonathan. (Nobody has been able to trace Russell). Meigui discovered Jonathan was involved in the blackmail and told him about Willie Wong's illness and together (apparently they are blaming each other) they bribed Willie with Stuart's blackmail money to commit his horrible act. Of course a lot of this is hearsay, but Happyfella's friend Inspector George Morton seems quite confident (with the help of modern day DNA) of putting them all in prison. Xiang Ju has returned to China and Mudan has had her passbook withheld whilst the death of her stepmother is being investigated, she is quite relaxed about it, she is staying with her father Yang Chang and they are making up for their lost years apart. Cathy and Beth have gone shopping – where else – Dublin to buy some shoes, Midge and I were at Chingford Mount Cemetery to see off my old friend Arthur. The whole gang is here, Nibbo, Downdrough Alfie, couple of S.PY.S. (South Poplar Youth) and Hijack. "How're you doing Hijack?" Nibbo said, "I must be mixing with the wrong people, I haven't had my lorry pinched for over a year!" said Hijack. "I wish someone would pinch my Misses." It was Grim, "Hello Grim," I said, adding, "What's the odds of Grim smiling today Nibbo?"

"We got more chance of England winning the Ashes!" said Nibbo.

Hijack came over to me and said, "Danny see that man over there don't, look quickly, the Chinaman with the Chinese woman, well, and he's the other man that I saw pushing Arthur into a car." I had a quick glance, and spoke to Midge, "Midge, Yang Chang, Hijack says he's the other guy pushing Arthur into the car."

"Leave it to me Danny." And off he went. As we made our way into the church, I looked back and saw a policeman talking to Yang Chang and, with Mudan, trying to stop the police; Yang Chang was pushed into a police car.

Arthur's coffin was carried in, placed gently at the front of the church.

The Vicar went through his normal service, and I had been asked by Cliff Rabinaue or "Rubbernose", Arthur's double act partner to make a speech, say a few nice words about Arthur. "Arthur and I go back a long time. It was only a short time ago that I remembered his real name. Of course before Arthur he was just called "A" Alexander. Arthur, he'll always be remembered as Arthur, what a double act, Arthur and Rubbernose/ Cliff Rabinaue, better than the two Ronnie's, and I don't mean Ronny and Reggie Kray. The last time I spoke to Arthur, Ron and Reggie's names came up. He told me off for being disrespectful, he said they were good clients of his and gave his firm a lot of work." That brought a few smiles through the tears, "When I was talking to him, I asked him how he became an accountant, he was always larking about when he was at school, you know, anything for a laugh. He answered that, being in the funeral game, he never took life seriously and when he grew up and became an accountant he carried on his Arthur act because it was his last chance of being a boy. And that's how I will always remember him, as one of the boys. Rubber asked me to do this, make this small speech. I said it should be him but he replied, "I only do a double Act!" I would just like to finish by saying, Arthur gave a lot of people a lot of laughs, and he was a special person and a hard act to follow."

I had to return to the office, we had to vote in a new replacement for Jonathan, and I wanted to clear the air and let them know what really happened, Rebecca, the companies secretary was waiting I asked her to sit and record the meeting. We spoke about Jonathan she was really shocked.

"Gentlemen, I have asked Rebecca to sit in and record this meeting. Gentlemen, in the absence of Mr Davidson-Smythe and now Yang Chang, I would like to try to let you know what is happening in the "Limehouse Link". As the link is not fully formed into the perfect chain, a) my link is being held as evidence by the police, you understand I was knocked out cold when I was hit with the Link.

And b) Yang Chang cannot attend, he has been arrested and the police believe they are going to charge him. I would also like to…" I stopped, "My apologies gentlemen. I think the honourable thingto do, following all the things happening on my patch, excuse the expression, and would be to resign."

Mr Wong looked at Yan Lee and Doo Ming before he spoke,

"Mr Holmes, could we ask you to wait outside to allow us to discuss what you have said to us?"

"Certainly Mr Wong." I replied and left the room. In less than five minutes Mr Wong called me to return.

"Mr Holmes, on behalf of Yin Lee, Doo Ming and myself, we would ask you to reconsider your resignation. We have known for some time some of what has been going on, Sue Wong being family, I am ashamed that Willy Wong was responsible for Mr Graham's death. That was a terrible thing to do to another person, it made things worse by receiving money. His families were told it was insurance money that they received. We checked that part of the story out and discovered he was not insured, indeed, he had been rejected." Mr Ming then spoke,

"You have our thanks for bringing it all to an end. We trusted Mr Davidson-Smythe until we found out about his other life, which would not have been a problem if it had been out in the open, in which case, he could not have been blackmailed.

Doo Ming was the next to talk.

"Mr Holmes, in the short time you have been with us, you have built up a reputation to be proud of. You're very good working with people, who, look upon you as being honest and fair, along with your hard work and integrity. This is what our organization is based on. Hard work and goodwill." Doo Ming sat down and Mr Wong got to his feet. "Mr Holmes, on behalf of my second cousin's family, the Wongs of Limehouse, who died in an accidental fire, I thank you for taking time out of you very special day, the day you got married, to drop off on the way to your wedding to show your respect and offer help to his family. They are ashamed of the way you have been treated and nearly died at the hands of people you trusted, whose name will never be mentioned in our family again."

"Please Mr Wong," I interrupted, "I know she's done wrong," I said holding my head that still hurt, "but forgive her, and realise that she was brought up in an environment where the master of the house, her father Wah Chang, had the responsibility of running a small empire. I am not judging his methods but it was in a very difficult, sometimes ruthless period, even resulting in beatings, of which I received, for no reason other than being what I am. I am not trying to offend you gentlemen but simply pointing out that the separate lives from the East to the West must have messed with her head."

"It's our way Mr Holmes, it would be foolish to discuss the rights and wrongs of our ancient customs, but I will leave it to somebody much younger than I, to change them," after a short interlude he continued, "We hope we can persuade you Mr Holmes to stay with us, we trust you implicitly, and suggest you could give it 3 to 4 months, then if you still feel the same then, you must do what is right for you and your wife."

"Thank you Mr Wong, I will do as you say, when I was first told about 'the Limehouse link' I was very excited, believe me it was not money on property Stuart left me in his will, money cannot buy you love, but 'The Limehouse link' brought a purpose in my life, but after a month, my life was put on hold, now I feel that life has a meaning again I look forward to a long and happy partnership,"

I went around the table shaking each one firmly by the hand. The meeting over I escorted them down to the main doors, we said our good byes and off they went. I returned to the Boardroom and sat down at the head of the table. Now after all that has gone on over the last year; I have come through it all. Now I am going to enjoy it all. Rebecca tapped on the door and looked in, "Good night Mr Holmes, I've locked up and put the minutes away."

"Good night and thank you." I said and sat back.

CHAPTER 7

LINK-UP

Are you like me? Do you miss the eye to eye, nodding, saying hello to complete strangers, getting into conversation, about the weather, football, west ham, I might as well stop there, they would not know who or where west ham is.

The meeting was an absolute flop, total disarray, waste of time. The company had employed a new legal accounting firm to fill the vacancy left by Jonathan. Davidson Smyth, who was awaiting trial for fraud, blackmail etc... etc... Jonathan had hidden nearly had all the files, which were of course most of the evidence, that would incriminate him, and here we were in New York, an incomplete chain, only three out of five gold links fitted together, but two short of making a perfect chain. Mr Yang Chang the Hong Kong link was in prison, waiting a murder trial and 'Doo Ming' 'the New York link, had mysteriously gone missing, so we could not hold a proper meeting until some of the mess is cleaned up. I was waiting for Midge Milren, an old mate, who just happens to a very good reporter, and this was a follow up story, midge being responsible to me being here in New York, or in fact, me being anywhere, if midge had not phoned the police in time, I would have been, in a vase, sitting on the mantelpiece, next to a photo of my idol, Bobby Moore.

Together Midge and I had successfully, although not entirely conclusively, discovered who and why Stuart Graham was murdered.

Stuart was my best mate when we were at school together, he had three step sisters, and Stuart's mum married the girl's father, when Stuart was 7 years old, the girl's mother and father having departed, when they were all very young. Mr Chang's, Stuart's stepfather, died in a fire when his restaurants kitchen burnt down with him inside, leaving his estate to Stuart's mum, who died by accident, falling down the stairs at the Greenwich subway under the Thames in London. Stuart was left a fortune and became 'the lime house link' and when Stuart was murdered in a bizarre sexual act, between him and Willy Wong both homosexuals, Stuart not knowing that Willy was dying from an aids virus, he left everything to me, 20% of the 'links' shares, named me as his successor, a million pound house in Chigwell, and 2,000,000 pounds in the bank.

I'd been sitting in this 'diner' for 45 minutes, waiting for Midge, who was 45 minutes late, the first thing I noticed is that there were quite a few Chinese client's, which accounts for Mr Ming, being a regular. And the reason we, when midge gets here, thought was the best place to start our enquiries, this being the last place Doo Ming was seen.

Midge came in mumbling, something about the freezing weather and brass monkeys.

"Would you believe I had trouble hailing a cab," said Midge, blowing into his hands, and adding "not the weather to go skinny dipping in"

"Not the weather to go walkabouts" I replied referring to Mr Ming's disappearance.

"What have we got Danny?" he asked.

"This was the last place, that he visited," I replied.

"The coffee not that bad is it?" he asked.

"Sorry Midge I'll order you one," and caught the eye of- I don't believe it.

There behind the counter was Meigui or her double, no, no what am I thinking. "Danny, are you alright? You look as if you have seen a ghost?" said Midge.

"Midge you see the lady behind that counter does she remind you of anyone?"

"Well, I'll be, a younger version, but the likeliness is extraordinary," said Midge and raising his hand, caught her attention, and with the finger pointing to me and them to him, ordered two coffees.

My eyes were on her every movement, the cheek bones, eye's, hair, even undoing and doing up her top button on her blouse; she did everything the same as Meigui.

"Midge, when she comes over with the coffees, don't say who I, or we are"

She came over with a tray, two coffees, and put down in front of us, I sat there, holding my breath, "Is there anything else you would like sir?" she asked quietly, "No thank you, eh, Rose" Midge answered, again pointing to her name pinned on her blouse.

She turned away, and returned to her work.

"Did you know that Rose is Meigui's in Chinese?" Midge said.

"Of course I bloody know," it too much of a coincidence Midge.

My mind was in a whirl; Meigui was my first love, form the age of eight or nine, Stuart, Meigui and I went everywhere together, playing in the bombed out streets of east London, growing up and finally falling in love, only to be warned off, by the Chinese family, who did not want Meigui to marry anyone but a Chinese man.

Her family even had me beaten up, and threatened worse, if I did not get out of Meigui's life.

I decided not to take any notice of them, but fate dealt with my wicked hand, and her majesty's army could not carry on without me, and I was called, conscripted into the army, and sent to Germany, when I returned Meigui was sent to china, and the next time we met was at Stuart's funeral.

Even after all those years we had rather strong feelings for each other, I suppose it's to do with first love, Meigui told me she had been married, but parted, also that she had two children, who live in China, I myself had loved Cathy for 15 years and then parted, but had since reunited and was now very happily married.

The last time that I had seen Meigui was the moment before she clouted me round the head, which is when Midge had phoned the police, to rush to my home in Chigwell, Essex just in time to stop Meigui's boyfriend, Goufan from injecting me with a lethal dose of drugs.

"Midge tell me that I'm not imagining things, they are like two peas in a pod, it must be her daughter," I said to Midge, putting my hands on my head, feeling the spot where Meigui had hit me, and remembering what the police had told me, she had been forced to get me, of course at that time, I was still recovering from the smash on the head and had had some drugs pumped into me by Goufan. Ever since, I had often wondered what made Meigui, hit me, I still thought that she cared for me a little, I had not seen her since her arrest, there had been no contact with Meigui, or her sisters.

"Are we just going to sit here all day Danny?" Midge was getting impatient "Happyfella's needs another fix (a front page exclusive)" he added.

I thought I would ask one of the china men sitting at the next table if they knew the whereabouts of a 'Doo Ming' but Midge beat me to it, and was already asking the questions.

"Just like you said Danny "Doo Ming was last seen here," and added "one of them said he seemed to be acting, out of character."

We called for the tag and Midge offered to pay, which meant I did not have to look 'Rose' in the eye, why that bothered me, I just didn't know, but I had a strange, odd kind of feeling.

We had arrived back at our hotel, having cleaned up I'd said that I had met in the bar, and have a couple of drinks before dinner, there was a knock on the door," Christ, you're early Midge," "What's up?" I asked seeing the look on his face.

"I don't know how to tell you this Danny, Cathy has left you," I usually joke when I'm nervous, I could not think of anything funny, but my hand automatically went for my mobile. "Beth put Cathy on please" she told me Cathy had given her phone to Beth, and had stormed off, without telling Beth what was wrong, and where she was going.

"What have you done to upset her Danny?" Beth asked, adding "I have never seen her so upset"

"Beth I'm coming home, on the next flight" Midge was staring at me "What's it all about Danny?" he asked "You will be the first one to know after me," I replied

We rushed down to their hotel reception, was directed to their travel counter, told her what we required, jumped on a cab to the airport. "Midge if you ask me again why she has left, I will jump from this plane," we were both getting edgy, the nearer we got to touchdown.

"I'll drop off first, if you don't mind, I'll let you know if Cathy has left you a note, I wish I know what was going on Midge, tell Beth I'll sort it all out."

"Call us a.s.a.p., now don't forget, best of luck Danny," the lights were on as I entered the house, so I called out "Is that you Cathy?"

"No it isn't, Mr Holmes, it's me" said Giovanna, our house keeper sounding quite annoyed, "Mrs Holmes has gone, she told me she will never forgive you for lying to her,"

"But I have not lied to her," I answered

"O, yes you have, and there's no denying it, she's got proof Mr Holmes," and with that Giovanna put on her coat and gave me her bunch of keys,"

"What are these for?" I asked

"I'm leaving as well" and left me standing by the door, too shocked to even ask why, and feeling very sorry for myself.

The next five days were awful, nobody was talking to me accept Midge, and he was away in 'Paris', and was very busy getting a fix (story) for Happyfella. Beth had decided not to speak to me, until Cathy and I had sorted things out. I wish I knew what was there to sort out, Cathy was not answering my phone calls, I'd asked Bath to pass on my messages, and I had to go to court, as a witness, at the trail of Meigui and her boyfriend Goufan.

The first day was terrible; there was Meigui standing across the courtroom next to her murdering boyfriend. Not once did she look at me, whilst the charges were read out, and she did not hesitate to the charges and never flinched, when her lawyer said guilty as charged, even after then her boyfriend claimed that he was acting under the influence of love, and then the threat of Meigui leaving him; he claimed that he had nothing against me, that he'd never met or even heard of me, until Meigui asked for his help to get rid of me.

This went on for 3 days, I was nearly sorry for the guy, I couldn't believe that Meigui hated me so much.

Midge arrived back from Paris and into the courtroom and sat down next to me.

After some more questions, Meigui agreed to every accusation levelled at her, the charges were read, by the judge, and the jury were told to retire and come to a verdict. And the court adjourned.

Midge caught the eye of my barrister, and beckoned him over, "Danny you will want to hear this," the barrister came over "I'm sorry to tell you this, but Meigui has been lying all the time, the so called boyfriend was holding Meigui's grandson, hostage, so she had to do as she was told," he handed some photos to the brief, who in turn, asked the judge if he could approach the bench, along with the other sides barristers retreated, the jury was recalled and the judge adjourned the case.

"What's going on Midge?" I asked.

"Just wait and I will tell you." He said.

"Cathy had a phone call from a boy claiming he had escaped from his captors, who was forcing his mother Meigui to lie, and take the blame for attempting to murder you," Midge said.

We cleared the court, along with all the crowd, Meigui was standing with the barristers, and a few other people, a lady was standing with her back to me and a Chinese lad of about 15 or 16 "Mr Holmes, I like to introduce you," the barrister beckoned.

I slowly moved towards them.

Meigui spoke, "Danny this is our daughter, 'Rose' and your grandson 'Daniel'

I was gob-smacked, the lady, our daughter turned and looked at me, it was the waitress from New York, the boy, my grandson, turned and looked at me, I was, unlike me, completely lost for words, Meigui said, "Danny I tried to tell you a hundred times, but when you went back to Cathy, I did not want to hurt you or her," she stopped and looked past me and I turned to see Cathy and Beth, they had heard what Meigui had said, in the next moment Cathy was in my arms. "Danny, Meigui please forgive me, when I received Daniel's phone call, I thought it was a hoax, you and Midge were in U.S.A, I was so angry, I just packed my bags and left, the next evening I decided to call midge's boss Jim Appicella who told me not to contact anybody. Daniel had given me a phone number, for me to contact him. I gave this to Jim, who phoned Midge, "Are they alright?"

"Cathy, I promise you, I did not know," Cathy let go of me and hugged Meigui, then her or our daughter, and kissed the boy softly on the cheek.

"Danny Holmes, I swear if you don't hug and kiss both your daughter and grandson, I'll set Beth on you," she said.

I hugged Meigui first and said "introduce me to my daughter and grandson," my daughter kissed me for the first time, my grandson shock me hand and hugged me, I had to shut my eyes, and thank god, and tears of joy fell down my face, "Beth, Midge, meet my grandson, the future 'lime house link.'"

'Grand-dad' the boy said looking at me, "can you take me to see my great grandmother's grave?" and my mind flashed back to the day Stuart was buried, and I thought of the saddest sight I had ever seen, the Hearst, the priest, had only one person. Sue Wong could now rest in peace.

So there we were, back at Chingford cemetery, of course "Wendy Long" had been removed from the gravestone, replaced by a new stone with "Sue Wong" name marked out across the top, with the words sadly missed by your lovely Daughters Meigui, Mudan, Xiag-ju, and your granddaughter rose, and great grandson Daniel.

There was not much said amongst the mourners, and after a time we started to disperse and made our way slowly, back towards the cars.

"You look puzzled," I said, walking alongside Midge, "You're not thinking what I'm thinking" I added. "Most likely I am "Midge said. "And asked "well, who did send the flowers, all the sisters said they did not know Wendy Long was Sue Wong?

The end.........

Printed in Great Britain
by Amazon

78970329R00092